Lipstick Like Lindsay's
and Other Christmas Stories

Lipstick Like Lindsay's

and Other Christmas Stories

GERALD R. TONER

PELICAN PUBLISHING COMPANY
GRETNA 1990

Library of Congress Cataloging-in-Publication Data

Toner, Gerald R.
  Lipstick like Lindsay's and other Christmas stories / by Gerald R.
Toner.
    p. cm.
  ISBN 0-88289-809-4
  1. Christmas stories, American. I. Title
PS3570.0484L57 1990
813'.54—dc20   90-36043
                                          CIP

Text illustrations by Joyce Haynes

Manufactured in the United States of America

Published by Pelican Publishing Company, Inc.
1101 Monroe Street, Gretna, Louisiana 70053

For Carol, Jennie, and John,
Who Give Life Its Meaning
and
In Memory of
John and Ruth
Who Gave Life in the
First Place

Contents

Preface

As you see it, *Lipstick Like Lindsay's and Other Christmas Stories* is a collection of ten contemporary Christmas stories which are both uplifting and real. There are no angels or big bang theatrics, but there are more than a few personal miracles that transpire in the course of these stories. Basically, I try to draw upon the ephemeral spirit of Christmas that pervades even the most cynical of us during the time between Thanksgiving and the New Year and illustrate through my words the way in which that spirit raises us all to a somewhat higher plane of being. My father, who had much of the "child" drummed out of him by the time he went to work after the eighth grade, often insisted emphatically that "Christmas is for the kids." I, just as emphatically, disagreed. Christmas is for everyone—child and adult alike—just as the first author of Christmas was for everyone, child and adult. These stories are not for little children, but they are addressed to the child-like beliefs in all of us.

Acknowledgments

First, I would like to thank Dr. Milburn Calhoun, for his foresight in perceiving the desire of American readers to celebrate the Christmas season *with* rather than simply *through* their children. Thanks also to my friend, Bill Schuetze, without whose intervention these stories would have never found their way to Pelican; and to Leo Burmester, who encouraged me to put them out before the public eye. A special thanks to Frank Capra, whose films inspired, and whose letters urged me to keep at it. Finally, my thanks to Pat Perry, Senior Editor of the *Saturday Evening Post*, who in 1986 took a chance on an unpublished and unrepresented attorney-writer.

Secondly, my thanks to friends who have read, critiqued, listened to, and experienced these stories as they came to life: Steve Vinsavich, Vince Staten, Charles Bracelen Flood, Pat Olson, Larry and Edith Ethridge, Mary Paynter, Jane Wehner, Rod Wilson, Geri Schubert, Judy Spalding, and Angela Blandford. Above all, thanks to my wife, Carol, for putting up with the manic-depression that comes with writing.

Lipstick Like Lindsay's
and Other Christmas Stories

THE CHRISTMAS VISITATION

J udge John Patrick O'Brien watched the December sky grow yellow, then orange as gray, snow-drenched clouds gathered from the west. The long afternoon was ending. It was O'Brien's last active day as judge of the Tenth Division Circuit Court. The last day he would watch the daylight disappear through the large modern windows that spanned his office in the new Hall of Justice. The last time he would decide a matter so seemingly insignificant as a little boy's visitation with his divorced parents.

It had been ten years since Judge O'Brien had made the move over from the old courthouse across the street. He had surrendered an office in which a future justice of the Supreme Court and a former U.S. senator had once grappled with the judicial issues of their day. Moreover, the office had thick oak paneling, a brass chandelier and, most memorably, a green leather couch his father had given him when he took the bench in 1955. His father had saved his Christmas bonus and then some to be able to afford that luxury for Patrick. It had been sacrificed when he was assigned the pristine nine-by-twelve cubicle in the new Hall of Justice. Perhaps with the couch, an era had passed for Judge O'Brien. The ten years after the move had marked a gradual slide in his judicial career, culminating in a November defeat the month before.

As his mind wandered back to the present O'Brien could feel the temperature dropping inside his office to match the cold front outside. The gray of the sky took over the last hint of daylight as the Judge's banjo clock struck five. O'Brien lifted his legs from his desk and lowered them to the floor. They were swollen more often now and tended to ache or fall asleep after a few moments. O'Brien looked at his calendar, running his right index finger carefully down the December dates until he arrived at Friday the 23rd.

After the election, he had determined to rest more often than not, take a full three weeks' vacation after Christmas, and simply not come back before his opponent took office. The one exception to this plan had been Dr. Grant's malpractice trial, which was to have begun in late November. O'Brien had intended that it be his judicial swan song. He had ordered pre-trial briefs, researched the law more thoroughly than he had in several years, and held pre-trial conferences on his own motion. Unwittingly, through his diligence he thus forced the litigants to come to their senses before the trial, and they settled the case. Nothing of any serious merit had arisen since that time.

O'Brien read the caption *Little v. Little* on his calendar. His brow furrowed, his bushy, unkempt eyebrows almost touching above his nose. That case had concluded six months before. Or had it? He remembered signing the final order. Or did he? He also remembered the subtle charges of his young opponent during the election. She said he was losing his edge. Admittedly, he tired more easily at sixty-five and dozed a little during the more boring cases, but certainly his mind was still sharp. He wrote few of his own decisions anymore, and his temper was somewhat shorter with attorneys who would not take "no" for an answer, but surely his memory was not failing. *Little v. Little* had concluded. He pushed the buzzer on his phone. There was no answer.

"Clarence," Judge O'Brien called out toward the hallway. There was a gentle rap at the door as Clarence responded. "Come in, Clarence." The black sheriff of the Tenth Division had been with O'Brien for as long as O'Brien had been on the bench.

"You called, your honor?"

"Clarence, glad you're here. I was beginning to think I was the only one around."

"No, your honor, I'm here." Clarence had always been there.

"Where's Peggy? I don't remember her telling me she was taking off early." His voice was as cautious as it was inquiring. He recognized his tendency to forget little things, and he knew that she had probably told him she was leaving early.

"I thought I heard her telling you the other day that she was going to the Bar Association Christmas party. You know it started around 4:30."

O'Brien winced. "Yes . . . yes, I do remember now. I must be getting a little foggy, but you know, I thought she'd at least say goodbye or something . . ."

It was Clarence's turn to wonder about his own memory. "Goodbye?"

"Yes, goodbye. It's my last day, you know."

"No . . . I didn't know. I take it you're not coming back in for the last few days before the new year?"

"That's right." O'Brien paused, then smiled faintly at his old friend. "And there was no reason for you to know. I didn't tell anyone."

"And why not?" Clarence's voice betrayed his pique at not being informed.

"I guess I just wanted to slide away. Forgo the cakes and gold watches." O'Brien fell silent for a moment. "Clarence?"

"Yes, your honor."

"Do you remember my old green couch? The one I used to have in the old courthouse?"

"Sure. The one with the big wide splits and the stuffing coming out!"

O'Brien laughed. Clarence's recollection was more realistic than his own idealized version of the abandoned couch.

"I remember the day my Daddy and I carried that old monstrosity up to the fourth floor of the old courthouse to my first office . . ."

"Yes, sir. They gave you the hottest, dingiest old hole-in-the-wall in the entire place . . ."

"And I loved it. I couldn't wait until Monday, so my Dad grabbed me on the Saturday before and he said, 'Patrick, you've got the key, so we're moving you in today.' And he got two men from the brewery where he worked, and we moved all my furniture in that day. When they left and my Dad and I were alone, we just stood there for a second and took it in. And then you know what my Dad did?"

"No, your honor."

"He hugged me, Clarence. My Dad turned around all sweaty and dirty and still breathing hard, and he hugged me." O'Brien turned his face away as a tear formed. Tears were not something O'Brien wanted on this particular day.

"Your Daddy was real proud of his boy." Clarence's statement was simple and direct. He, too, wanted to avoid a scene, so he groped for another topic. "Say, I'll bet Katie and her husband are coming in for Christmas . . . celebrate the grand retirement . . . big turkey . . ."

"No . . . no. It's *his* family's turn this year. I get them New Year's weekend." Looking down at his desk, he saw the troublesome note on his calendar.

"Clarence, why do I have *Little v. Little* on my book for this afternoon? Why do I have anything on my calendar for this afternoon? We should both be at the Bar Foundation Building sipping egg nog."

"Well, your honor, Peggy scheduled the hearing. It was the only available time. It's a Christmas visitation question."

"Good God," O'Brien muttered in disgust. "She should have known better than that. She knows how I've always hated these family questions . . . no law . . . flip a coin . . . everyone leaves angry."

"Well, Judge, if you please, I was talking to the boy's grandma out in the courtroom. She and the boy got here early. And according to her . . ."

"Clarence, you know I'm not supposed to listen to ex parte discussions."

"You're right, Judge."

"Well, never mind. You were saying that she told you . . ."

"She told me the boy's been with her for a couple of weeks now. Seems her son, the boy's daddy, travels a lot and so does the boy's mother, and now they both want the boy for Christmas."

"Okay, I probably shouldn't listen to any more before we go out in the courtroom." O'Brien paused. "Does the boy appear to be abused?" The judge had been instructed to always inquire. An affirmative response might prompt him to refer the case to child services and get him out of the courthouse before five thirty.

"No. His grandma's been treating him fine, and I suspect his Mom and Dad love him a lot; he's okay."

"Oh . . ." O'Brien sighed, rising slowly from his chair and straightening his back. "Let's get on with it, then." O'Brien walked stiffly to the peg behind his office door and reached for the black robe he had worn for the last thirty years. By second nature Clarence helped him into the robe, neither man realizing at that point it was a ritual not to be repeated.

O'Brien moved out into the hallway, now dark and deserted, raised his robe slightly and, leaning over the water fountain, took three quick swallows to remove the dry, cottony feeling from his mouth. "Okay, Clarence, let's go." Both men paused for a moment, now cognizant of an era which was ending.

Clarence smiled, then swung open the door and strode into the courtroom. "All rise. Hear ye. Hear ye. Silence is commanded. Judge John Patrick O'Brien of the Jefferson Circuit Court, Tenth Division is now presiding. All ye who have motions to be heard shall be heard. Be seated and remain silent."

Judge O'Brien walked forcefully into the courtroom and stepped up to the bench. A file sat unopened in front of him. He looked up and briefly greeted the parties and their counsel. There was no need to delve very deeply into the contents of the file. It was there more for security than any real purpose. Judge O'Brien vaguely remembered Mr. and Mrs. Little and their attorneys, Ms. Stryker and Mr. Stall. In the back of the courtroom sat a little boy—maybe seven or eight— huddled closely to an older woman, who, he supposed, was the grand-mother. It was the first time he had actually seen the Little's child. His eyes reverted to the file in front of him and he skimmed the motion of the mother's attorney.

"Mr. Stall," O'Brien began. "Your motion to change Christmas visitation is before the court. Could you please familiarize the court briefly with the facts and basis for your motion." O'Brien surprised himself with the apparent solemnity of his demeanor.

Stall stood up and cleared his throat, glancing nervously at the sheriff, then opposing counsel, and at last the judge. He and Ms. Stryker both realized that they were before the wrong judge on the wrong day at the wrong hour of the afternoon.

"If the court please, your honor. We will try to be brief, knowing that we all want to get home on this Friday before Christmas." Stall paused. He was never brief and often irrelevant. "As you may recall my client, Mrs. Little, was granted custody of her eight-year-old son, Patrick, in the decree you entered earlier this year." O'Brien's eyes softened. He had never known the boy's name was Patrick. "The visitation agreement that was reached between the parties and the court provided that the boy spend Thanksgiving from Wednesday through Sunday with his mother and that he spend Christmas from December twenty-first through December twenty-sixth with his fa-ther. Well, it seems that his mother . . . uh, the former Mrs. Little . . ." Stall cleared his throat a second time. O'Brien was constantly amazed at the manner in which Stall always cleared his throat just before making a slight misstatement of fact. ". . . had a business engagement in California over Thanksgiving weekend. So she obtained a tradeoff with Mr. Little for Christmas."

"She went skiing and dumped him on me," Mr. Little murmured loudly.

O'Brien cracked his gavel down. "Ms. Stryker, you will please advise your client to remain silent until the court asks him a question and to otherwise address the court through counsel."

"Yes, of course, your honor. We're sorry," Stryker explained with a withering glance at Mr. Little.

Stall continued. "The boy, Patrick, has been with his father's mother for the past two weeks, and in the interests of the child, it would seem advisable that he spend Christmas with his mother, the custodial parent. You see, we believe that the interests of justice demand . . ."

O'Brien looked around him as Stall blabbered on. In the old courtroom the ceilings had been twenty feet high with fourteen-inch crown molding, and the plaster walls were adorned with portraits of the Commonwealth's past Circuit Judges. The new courtroom had eight-foot ceilings, with recessed fluorescent lighting and concrete walls . . . so much like a prison. More importantly, there had been a time when domestic relations had been handled by the chancery courts and assigned to commissioners.

Judge John Patrick O'Brien gazed to the back of the courtroom. He rubbed his chin, striking a pose that made it appear that he was deep in thought, contemplating the question before him. It was an acquired skill. Then something—the boy's squirming or the pained expression on the old woman's face—caught his attention. O'Brien suddenly knew that his decision would make a difference, and it made him all the more uncomfortable.

Clearing his throat and adjusting his horn-rimmed glasses, Judge O'Brien looked to the tables of both counsel. Fully aware of the answer to his question, O'Brien asked, "Who are the visitors at the back of the courtroom?"

Ms. Stryker stood up. "Your honor, that's the boy and his grandmother, Mr. Little's mother. If you would like we can have them leave the room."

"Mr. Stall, would you prefer that they leave the courtroom?"

"Well, no, your honor, but perhaps it would be better if . . ."

"Very good. If there are no objections, then the court will ask them to stay."

Ms. Stryker stood up and began to speak. "Just a minute, counselor," O'Brien interrupted. "Please introduce our visitors to the court. Better still, Mrs. Little, would you and your grandson please come down a few rows." Ms. Stryker eased back into her seat. O'Brien was living up to his reputation as being just a little abrupt and more than a little eccentric.

"I understand Patrick's been with you for a few weeks, Mrs. Little?" O'Brien continued.

The older woman stood up. "Yes, your honor. I live close to his school and I'm retired now, so Patrick and I can get together and play when school's over." She stopped, embarrassed that she had begun to talk too much.

"Do you drive, Mrs. Little?"

"Drive? No . . . I mean I suppose I could . . . but I just don't. I guess we don't need to very much."

O'Brien liked the woman before him. She had spunk and a mind of her own. But he also knew he had to test her.

"If you don't drive, how do you arrange for Patrick to get around to activities and such? I mean, does he have after school activities?"

"Why, of course he does, your honor. But Patrick can walk or ride his bike most places. When he can't, we've never had any trouble getting a ride."

"Thank you, Mrs. Little. You may sit down. And Patrick, what have you been doing to get ready for Christmas?"

"Oh, buying presents and fixing the tree and making bread and stuff with grandma."

"You have a lot of fun with your grandma, don't you?"

"You bet, your honor."

"But does that give you time to get outside and play?"

"Oh sure, there are lots of kids in our," Patrick's voice fell with his gaffe, "I mean my grandma's neighborhood."

"How's school going for you, Patrick?" O'Brien knew he had better explore the adequacy of Patrick's education for the record. "Keeping up a B average?"

"No, sir! A−. . . except for conduct."

O'Brien laughed. "I knew a boy like that once, Patrick. . . ." Memories of his own school days flooded over him. "You may sit down now, son."

The judge turned his eyes back to Mr. Stall. "Mr. Stall, where will your client and her son be going for the Christmas holidays?"

Stall beamed, certain that the judge's question was a precursor to quick victory. "Perhaps Patrick's mother might best inform the court . . ."

"Yes, that would be fine. Mrs. Little . . . that is, the ex-Mrs. Little . . ." Judge O'Brien hated the stumbling over once, and sometimes future, names.

"Well, your honor, I have a friend in New York City, and . . . uh . . . Patrick and I were going there."

"And *he* lives in Manhattan? Your friend, that is?"

The former Mrs. Little glanced nervously at Mr. Stall. "Yes . . . well, he has a very nice town house that overlooks Central Park."

"I see. And does he have a Christmas tree?"

"Well, I don't know. I never asked him."

The judge smiled solicitously. "And space? I mean, Patrick will have, or I should say . . . *would* have Central Park and all to play in . . ."

Patrick's mother wondered if this was a test. "Well, I'm not sure that would really be all that good of an idea . . ."

"But Patrick would have quality time, wouldn't he? I mean, when you were actually *with* Patrick you could go out. Maybe see Rockefeller Center?"

"Well, yes, I suppose we could." Her answer was tentative, cautioned as she was by Mr. Stall to watch for traps. "I mean, there is a lot going on during the holidays."

"I see, Mrs. Little . . . thank you." O'Brien paused, collecting his next series of questions. "And Mr. Little, how are you going to be spending Christmas?"

Ms. Stryker stood up. "If I may speak for my client, your honor . . ."

The judge's stare silenced her. "Ms. Stryker, please, if you don't mind. We can speak informally in this forum, particularly at the court's request. Mr. Little may address the court directly."

Mr. Little stood up. His anger and bravado had dissolved. "Well, your honor, I have an apartment here in town. I'll probably be staying here. Have some friends over. You know . . . the usual parties, some folks from the office, the guys . . ."

"And the girls?" the judge added, with more than a touch of sarcasm.

"Well . . . yes . . . of course . . ."

"Just an intimate little party?"

"Well, your honor, the office crowd is pretty big, come to think of it. You know . . . I mean . . . you know . . ." The judge raised his hand to both calm and silence the flustered Mr. Little.

"Yes, I think I do know." His eyes diverted to Patrick's grandmother. "Mrs. Little." Instinctively Patrick's mother started to stand up. "No, I'm sorry . . . not you, Mrs. Little . . . I mean Patrick's grandma." The older woman nodded. "You said you live near Patrick's school. Where exactly is that, and what is Patrick's school?"

"Irish Hill, your honor. Payne Street. Patrick attends St. Aloysius."

O'Brien knew the neighborhood well. It was old, ethnic and working class. So Patrick's father, the finely tailored stockbroker, had at least been more down to earth at some point in his life.

Stall interrupted. "Forgive me, your honor, but the boy's mother is contemplating a move out of town after the first of the year. So the boy will obviously be leaving St. Aloysius."

"Yes . . . I see," O'Brien said quietly. He glanced at the clock on the wall. It was past 5:30. The party was almost over. He needed to reach a decision. A finding for either litigant would quickly resolve things; the anger would simply carry over to another judge, another day, another dispute.

"Well, Mr. Stall, I have to recognize that your client is the custodial parent. She is the boy's mother. Certainly, visitation is merely a privilege Mr. Little enjoys."

"Thank you, your honor." Stall beamed with victory.

The judge ran his hand back through his hair and pressed his glasses off of his nose and against his temple.

"On the other hand, Mr. Little has certain parental rights. Christmas was scheduled as his time."

O'Brien balked for a moment. Suddenly, and for no particular reason, he realized that this would be his last decision on the bench. It would not be the type of legal analysis that had once been his pride. Training at the state university and Harvard Law School had not prepared him for such an arbitrary decision.

"Mr. Little," O'Brien again addressed the litigant directly, "have you a Christmas tree in your apartment?"

Little turned and looked at his lawyer. She looked back at Mr. Little helplessly.

"Mr. Little?" O'Brien repeated.

"Well, no. Frankly, his mother and I both believe that Patrick's getting a little too old . . . well, he's sufficiently mature . . . that it doesn't . . . or isn't necessary."

Judge O'Brien interrupted. "Please, Mr. Little, I was just curious. The court is instructed by statute to be aware of and consider foremost the interests of the child. This alone certainly doesn't determine whether you or your former wife would best provide for the child's well-being at Christmas."

"Mrs. Little," O'Brien continued his questioning, "have you social plans for Christmas Eve and if so, will you be able to make sitter arrangements?"

"Yes, your honor. Patrick's sitter will be a very bright girl—my friend's oldest daughter."

"Thank you, Mrs. Little, I'm sure that the arrangements will be adequate."

Judge O'Brien stood up abruptly. The prerogative of the court required no explanations. "The court will take a very brief recess. Please remain in the courtroom."

The judge raised his robes and walked with uncommon speed out of the courtroom. He stepped into the back hall, felt the sweat on his upper lip, and leaned over the drinking fountain, taking the water in gulps.

"What are you going to do, Judge?"

O'Brien started. It was Clarence, standing by his side with folded arms. The two of them were the only representatives of the State remaining in the Hall of Justice.

"Clarence, I don't know. Decisions like this shouldn't be made by judges. The law tells me I have two choices—father or mother—and neither will help that boy very much. Not that they are bad parents really. They're just a little selfish and still very angry at each other." He paused. "I hate this part of it."

"The boy's happy with his grandma, Judge," Clarence interjected. "I saw them outside together before the hearing. They were playing and cutting up and hugging and kissing on each other."

"Clarence, I'm sure you're right. I can see that, too. But I have no legal right to do anything but choose between the parents. Besides, the grandma is Mr. Little's mother. Like it or not, he'd have the boy within moments."

They stood in helpless silence together. The judge had no legal precedent, no worries about his professional pride, and no ready solution; he simply wanted a just result. Following "the book" was neither possible, since the decision to choose between mother and father lay within his judicial discretion, nor was it desirable. Reversal by the Court of Appeals would no longer bruise his ego—his days of worrying about reputation were over. This was how his career would end—on a Friday before Christmas, trapped within a miserable decision that could offer no legal swan song nor newspaper headline.

The judge suddenly pictured his final trip from the courthouse. He could imagine the snow that must now be falling outside his window, gradually making the downtown streets more treacherous and desolate. He could see the lonely winding way up the drive to the rambling Victorian house he had made into a home, and an image—brief, yet piercing—of his father at Christmas, poised before the tree where it had always stood, holding out his arms. "Patrick O'Brien, you rascal, come here."

The old judge twisted his head away from Clarence, overcome for a moment by the memory.

He felt a nudge on his arm. "Come on, Judge. You'll do the right thing. You always have." Clarence started to move away.

"Wait, Clarence . . . do you really mean that?" O'Brien asked.

"Why sure I do, your honor. Everybody knows that."

Judge O'Brien was stunned. Clarence was sincere. A feeling that had left him long before the last election now began to edge its way back into O'Brien's consciousness. O'Brien had once felt that he made the "right" decisions. Perhaps, even after his own confidence had waned, his decisions had remained sound. He took a deep breath, then straightened up.

"Come on, Clarence, let's get on with this and get home." O'Brien reached for the door and grasped the brass bar tightly. "Let's see if we can bring some justice to light."

Judge O'Brien quickly took the bench and brought the gavel down with authority. "Court is in session." Clarence grinned. There was something in O'Brien's voice that reminded him of years past.

"Would Patrick's grandmother please step forward?"

The old woman looked at the little boy, and he moved over suddenly to her, hugging her tightly.

"I'll be all right," O'Brien heard her whisper. She came to the front of the courtroom.

"Mrs. Little, are you married?"

"Widowed, your honor."

"I see." O'Brien nodded. "How often have you seen Patrick in the last three years?"

". . . Oh, your honor, Patrick's been with me quite a bit—several times a week."

"And steadily for the past two weeks, Mrs. Little?"

"Yes, your honor."

"Please take a seat, Mrs. Little."

O'Brien folded his hands and looked squarely at the parties and their lawyers.

"The court has heard the evidence and considered the file. Under ordinary circumstances the court must find for the boy's mother." Stall grinned as the judge paused. His grin eroded as O'Brien continued. "But these are not ordinary circumstances." Stryker began to twitch her fingers in nervous anticipation.

"The court declines to grant custody to either Mr. or Mrs. Little. Recognizing that the court has no right to grant custody to Patrick's grandmother, the court will hereby turn Patrick over to the County Youth Authorities until the court can decide this question *after* Christmas recess." O'Brien looked solemnly at Clarence, then smiled knowingly. "However, since the County Youth Advocate has gone home—or to a party—the court will turn Patrick over to the court bailiff, who will in turn see that the boy is retained in the custody of the court. Now, it so happens that the court is spending Christmas at home, with Patrick and his grandmother—if she will be my guest—and the court's phone will be open for calls and the court's living room will be open for visits from either Mr. or Mrs. Little if time permits. It is so ordered."

The gavel came down and in unison the lawyers bounced up with objections. The litigants shot angry glances as Judge O'Brien calmly gathered his robes and left the bench. Clarence, beaming ear to ear, turned one last time towards the litigants, lawyers, and guests.

"Court is now adjourned! Merry Christmas to everyone!"

Patrick's parents left the courthouse, unified at last, muttering of injustice and the senility of the judge. Patrick and his grandmother waited patiently on the front steps, where Clarence had asked them to meet the judge. Judge O'Brien quietly shed his robes, never to be worn again, and as he looked out his window at the snowflakes swirling and dancing in the street below, he smiled with satisfaction as he turned off his office light for the last time. The case would never be reported in the books. No law school professor would follow it like a text. But for John Patrick O'Brien, who had stretched the letter of the law into a shape more closely resembling justice, not only had the question of a child's visitation been decided, but the decision itself had visited upon him the spirit of Christmas . . . and that spirit would dwell with him for the rest of his days.

LIPSTICK LIKE
LINDSAY'S

I n the fourth century, when the tales and memory of Christ were still young, there lived a man named Nicholas who was bishop of the city of Myra in Lycia, Asia Minor. History has it that he was persecuted and martyred by Emperor Diocletian. Thereafter he became the patron saint of children, remembered for the gifts he left in secret in memory of Christ's birth. While much about his life is legend, his custom of giving gifts is a fact, and it is a custom that has without fail been entrusted to willing disciples throughout the centuries.

Under such a discipleship, and acting under St. Nicholas's guidance, I hoisted my daughter to my knee and inquired as to her secret list for Christmas. I take this assignment from St. Nicholas seriously. I always have.

Jennie spoke directly and to the point.

"I want crayon lipstick like Lindsay Schell's."

"What else would you like?"

Jennie thought long and hard. She was only four years old and had not learned the words "BMW" or "mink." In fact, it became very clear that she had thought long and hard in anticipation of this moment of list making, and the "crayon lipstick like Lindsay Schell's" was not only paramount, it was exclusive. I suggested a few odds and ends and we sealed the letter to St. Nicholas with love and kisses.

27

Jennie's discovery of the crayon lipstick in question had been for-tuitous. She knew about real lipstick, of course, and about play lipstick that was barely visible to the naked eye and totally innocuous to the keeper of a child's clothes. But this was a look-like-a-crayon-deep-colored-apparently-harmless-and-supposedly-hypo-allergenic stick of chemicals that spread like real lipstick. Lindsay, age six and more worldly wise, had come to the house one night for pizza with her mother and father and shared her lipstick with Jennie. From that point on it became a fixed object on Jennie's wish list.

I was, at first, amused and delighted. God's miracles come, on occasion, in small packages, and I knew that one day Jennie might develop a similar fervor for more expensive gifts. Thus, for this year, Jennie's wishes and Santa Claus's orders to myself were commensurate with my budgetary constraints. The crayon lipstick could not possibly cost more than $2.50. In short, an easy task had been laid out for St. Nicholas, and therefore myself as his agent.

My wife urged me not to delay. She was wise, and I was not. A few weeks passed. The memory of Thanksgiving faded into December and Christmas preparations. Work at the office took on a double-time cadence as every attorney in town tried to pack the month of December into its first two weeks, knowing that the only thing that would be packed in the last two weeks would be the bags of every attorney in town. It was the fifteenth of the month before I began to catch up with the joy of the season.

We bought our tree, and Jennie spoke about "crayon lipstick like Lindsay Schell's." We finished our Christmas cards and began reading our favorite Christmas stories, and Jennie giggled in anxious antici-pation of a "crayon lipstick like Lindsay Schell's." We lit our Advent candles, and I could tell that she was dreaming not of sugar plums but of crayon lipstick. I smiled, knowing that St. Nicholas would allow me to fulfill that desire at any of a dozen drugstores, department stores, and even supermarkets within two miles of our home.

And then one early evening, after a medical deposition in the vicinity of numerous shopping centers, I decided to make a quick trip to the local Children's Palace and swiftly accomplish my assign-ment. Through most of the year, the roads which lead through the chaos of shopping center land are merely an endless array of erratic lights and signs. At Christmas time, they become a snarling mass of harried Christmas shoppers. Inching my way through the traffic to the correct curb cut for Children's Palace, I turned in just as a steady downpour erased all possible visibility through my windshield.

It will rain from here on in. All the way to Christmas. That is not literary license. It just happened that way. It rained and didn't seem to stop. If it did stop it was while I was asleep or in the office. If I made the slightest move for the door or got into my car to drive anywhere it would start raining.

I found the only parking place available, having hovered about the lot for what seemed a modest eternity. Typical fortune found me about ten yards from the expressway and sixty yards from the front door of the store without an umbrella. I sighed, "Such are the wages of virtue," rolled up my pants a turn or two, thrust open the door, and puddle jumped to the entrance of the toy store.

Inside the store, a light steam rising off of my suit, I began wandering up and down the aisles in search of either the play makeup or an employee. Since all employees in discount stores are either on break or disguised as customers, I found the play makeup first. They had Tinkerbell, Bo-Po, Barbie, and numerous other concoctions, but no crayon lipstick.

After a modicum of stealth, I trapped an unsuspecting employee and asked her for the crayon lipstick. I carefully described the object of my search and slowly, as "through a glass, darkly," she showed a glimmer of recognition.

"Yeah. We had that."

"Great," I replied, trying to ignore her use of the past tense, "where is it?"

No one in this position ever gives a completely straight answer. She responded, "It was on aisle thirteen."

"I looked on aisle thirteen, and it's not there," I began, "but maybe if you'll come with me, we'll find it. I probably just didn't see it." I have learned that a plea of stupidity will often work wonders in such instances. She smiled and nodded and we walked together to aisle thirteen.

"It used to be there," she said. "But we must have sold out."

"Could you check for me?" I asked.

"Hey, Margie," she called out. An older woman emerged from a wall of boxed big wheels where she had been hiding. "This man wants to know if we got any play lipsticks."

Before I could interrupt, Margie had educated me as to the various other lipsticks that could be found on aisle thirteen. I then noted politely that I was searching for a specific crayon lipstick like Santa Claus had brought Lindsay the year before. She noted that Jennie would not know the difference. I assured her that Jennie would.

"Well, we had them. But they sold out. I don't know if we'll be getting any more in before Christmas or not."

There was really nothing more to say. I thanked them, and thinking to myself that I had just dried out, I went back into the rain. "This might be a little harder than I thought," I told myself as I hugged the wall of the building in a futile attempt to avoid the downpour, and went around the corner to Service Merchandise.

I was no more fortunate in the home of catalogue sales. "I remember those. They looked liked crayons. Real popular a while back."

"Right," I said eagerly.

"We don't have 'em."

"Gonna get 'em back?"

"I couldn't say. You never can tell."

I went on to the Walgreen's drug store next door.

"Crayon lipstick?" I believe the woman thought I was a little odd.

"It's for Christmas . . . my little girl," I said.

"Try aisle five."

I tried aisle five and found only real lipstick. Evidently she hadn't believed my story about Christmas and my little girl. I checked aisle seven for toys and found only the usual collection of non-crayon, and therefore inferior, children's play makeup.

I made my way back to the car, got in, and turned on the radio, only to have the newscaster remind me that it was December 17, "just seven shopping days left before Christmas." I pulled the car back into what is euphemistically referred to as the "flow of traffic," but which was at the moment actually more like a trickle or a drip, and worked my way down the strip.

An inconsequential errand, casually made on the heels of a deposition, had not gone at all as expected. Rather than leave well enough alone for the time being, I stopped at Thornbury's, the oldest toy store on the strip, knowing that I would pay a lot more, but confident that I would find what I wanted. While the young girl was far more interested in my request, she had even less help to offer. She knew what I wanted, but they hadn't stocked the item for weeks—maybe months.

The word "months" sent a sudden chill through me. What if I had not just run into a streak of bad luck, but an outright famine? I walked away from Thornbury's Toys with growing concern. They hadn't even suggested a place I might purchase a stick of crayon lipstick.

I glanced at my watch and noticed it was almost seven. Already late for dinner, I headed down the road for home, determined that the next day would bring better luck. Then, like a gambler drawn to that one last slot machine prime for the plucking, I noticed the Woolworth's sign over to my right. "Well, why not," I asked myself, signaling quickly and pulling into a space.

The store was everything a dime store should be. Musty, dusty, and old, it was the type of place that still sold rubber spoolies for women's hair. It was perfect for my purposes. I went straight to the manager.

"Do you have . . . or have you carried . . . a type of play lipstick that looks like a crayon?"

"Sure," he said. Here was a man's man. A giant among men. A hero from his clip-on tie down to the pointed ends of his shoes. "They're right back here." And he personally led me to a pegboard at the back of the store.

Our eyes searched the pegboard together. There was an ominous metal hook that was empty. He didn't have to tell me, but he did anyway.

"They *were* right there."

"But you sold out the last one a week or so ago," I offered.

"That's right." He smiled. "But the other stores might have some left."

"Could you check?"

"I'll be glad to," he said. And with that, he initiated a series of phone calls, during which I found that Woolworth's was closing its stores in the area. All of their stock had, in fact, been moved to Lexington. But they did remember the crayon lipstick.

"I'm awful sorry I couldn't help," he said. I knew that he was sincere and thanked him for his help and his sincerity. My way home was filled with a grim determination shadowed by slowly increasing panic.

I laid the situation out to my wife and she stated that which I already knew.

"You started too late, sweetheart."

"You are right," I said with a certain amount of hurt pride. "But do you have any ideas?"

"Keep trying drug stores and dime stores."

"I will," I said. "I will," I mumbled to myself. And the next day I began the phone calls.

I started with the remaining toy and discount stores. An entire morning of otherwise billable hours was spent in large part "on hold" while the search for the elusive lipstick was made. I have no idea whether they all searched their counters and shelves or stood around waiting for the light on the phone to go out so they could go back on break. But I never hung up. And finally a pleasant enough woman at a Target Department Store acknowledged my request, telling me she was familiar with the product and that she had it in the store. My excitement knew no bounds.

I made my excuses at the office and slipped away during lunch. The store was a good fifteen minutes away by car and under normal circumstances I would never have made the trip. By now, of course, these were not normal circumstances. And I was glad to give up lunch if I met with success.

I didn't. I searched the Target Store and found neither lipstick nor helpful employee. My informant had been ill-informed and I had been led astray. I ate a Hershey bar for lunch as I drove back to the office.

On Thursday night Jennie and I were in the kitchen making cookies when the phone rang. I answered. I could tell it was long distance. "May I speak with a little girl named Jennie?" I knew immediately it was the Boss himself, the man in charge, in two words: Santa Claus. I gave the phone to Jennie.

"Hello. Yes, this is Jennie." There was a pause, then a giggle of delight. She cupped her little hand over the receiver. "It's Santa Claus, Daddy," she whispered.

"I know," I whispered back. For the past two years, my special contacts with St. Nicholas had prompted this annual phone call. It was made from a friend's house in Cincinnati, one hundred miles away.

I kept stirring the oats into the batter as I listened to her conversation.

"Yes, I've been a good girl . . ." another pause while I held my breath, "I want a crayon lipstick just like Lindsay Schell's." My heart sunk. The conversation had quickly taken on the tenor of a conspiracy. If ever I have wished that the cup would be passed on to a more worthy agent of St. Nicholas, it was at that moment. Jennie ended her conversation, aglow with the magic of Christmas.

The next morning I took desperate measures. First, I called Carol Schell, Lindsay's mother. I explained my dilemma.

"Carol, could you look at Lindsay's lipstick and give me the name of the manufacturer?"

"Of course," she said, immediately responding to the shrill edge of abject fear in my voice. "But I'll have to find it first."

"I'll wait," I replied. And I waited, until Carol returned to the phone several minutes later.

"Are you still there?"

"Where else?" I laughed, ignoring the mounting stack of return phone slips which my secretary was dutifully placing before me.

"I've got it. Have you got a pencil and paper?"

"You bet," I responded, and meticulously repeated and copied the information.

When I had thanked Carol and hung up, my secretary came in and stood at the end of my desk. She looked at me and smiled warmly.

"I overheard what you were doing. You are a very special daddy."

"If I were really a special daddy," I said, "I wouldn't be in this fix now."

"Hmmm," she said, and handed me a piece of paper with the Manhattan area code written on it.

I got the number and tried to remain calm as the receptionist answered.

"Hi, my name is . . . well you don't care about that, but you see, I'm a lawyer . . . and . . ."

"You want the legal department?" she interrupted.

"No, no . . . I want . . . uh . . . your consumer ombudsman."

"Just a moment," she responded. I was momentarily impressed with my ability to move right to the source of all knowledge. That apparent skill, however, was soon outdistanced by my persistence. Three more departments and ten minutes later, I finally stumbled onto the appropriate party.

"Yes," the woman said with a heavy north Jersey accent, "I am familiar with that product. Did you say you are a lawyer?" I noted caution in her voice.

"Yes, I am . . . but please, this isn't business. I just want a stick for my little girl. I'll pay for you to Federal Express it . . ."

"Oh . . ." she laughed. "Four years ago we sold millions of those lipsticks. You know how fads go, though. Two years ago the market dwindled to nothing. We dropped the stuff. Listen, you don't want last year's news. This year it's glitter stickers. You can get 'em everywhere!"

Her words hit like the proverbial ton of bricks.

"But Jennie doesn't want what every kid wants this year. You don't have maybe a few sticks left . . . you know . . . for old times' sake?"

"Take my word," she replied, "they're out . . . o-u-t out!"

"Right, well, thanks for the information." I hung up. The big "NO" had come from the "Big Apple," and I realized that I was in considerable trouble.

That night my wife and I regrouped. She was the first to deal with the problem head on.

"I'd say you are up the well-known creek," she said.

"I'd say you are right," I said.

"Well," she began after a pause, "maybe we should just let Jennie know in a note that Santa Claus tried as hard as possible, but that we can't always get everything we want."

"That's fine for Jennie," I chuckled weakly, though I knew it wouldn't be fine for Jennie, "but what about me?"

She looked at me solemnly, realizing for the first time how deeply this test of my traditional principal-agent relationship with St. Nicholas had cut to my core. The conversation drifted, and I began to compose in my mind the note explaining why there would be no crayon lipstick like Lindsay Schell's.

Officially, the search ended that night. I am, after all, an adult of sorts. To anyone who asked at the office, I adhered to the party line: you can't have what isn't available.

Secretly, I continued to pursue every possible avenue as the days moved all too quickly toward Christmas. I called my sister in Cincinnati and my mother-in-law in Birmingham. After a few pleasantries I got to the point, mercilessly shaming myself and offering eternal gratitude if they could find the lipstick in Ohio or Alabama. They tried, but my operatives met with no success.

On my way to see a client in Frankfort I purposely took the long way through Shelbyville, hoping to myself that one of the old, small-town drug stores ignorant of the outdated nature of the stuff might have some of the crayon makeup left on a dusty shelf.

"We had some, dear," said the jolly little lady with the purple rinse in her hair, "but we sold out."

"I know," I said with resignation. "I didn't really think you'd have any." She showed me another, very nice lipstick, but I knew it would never do. I was twenty minutes late for my meeting, and I said I had been delayed by "business." As Marley said to Scrooge, "mankind was my business."

My efforts became calmer, more fatalistic. On December 23, when I went into the old Woolworth's that still remained in downtown Lexington, I was almost as amused as they when I revealed that I knew some of their stock had been shipped over from Louisville.

"How did you know?"

"Oh, I get around," I said, feeling a little like a Fuller brush man. "Now, about the crayon lipstick . . ."

Like the kind man in Louisville, the lady walked me to the aisle where it had been and was no more. I thanked her and walked back into the rain. For it was still raining.

I finished my business and headed north out of town. I mentally reviewed my efforts and realized that I had covered more square miles in my search for the perfect present than during any other Christmas. I also realized that I had failed. The drizzle, which continued in a light but steady stream, fit my mood perfectly.

It was not the nature of the gift that prompted my frustration, nor my failure to attain its purchase that fed my melancholia. In years past, and I was sure in years to come, I had reminded and would remind myself and my family—Jennie and, later, my son John foremost—that the greatest gift which St. Nicholas would have us give or receive in Christ's name would be our love. Certainly baseball gloves, dollhouses, fur coats, gold jewelry, or even automobiles are merely second-class attempts at showing that love. The wise men knew that even as they came forth with their frankincense, gold and myrrh.

It was more a sense of a failed entrustment that overcame me. St. Nicholas had made me the trustee for his simple little gift to Jennie, and I felt like I had somehow breached my fiduciary duty to both of them. I knew in my head that my wife's recommendation of a note explaining the lipstick's absence would be a helpful passage to maturity, but in my heart there was no solace for failure.

These were my thoughts as I shifted into fifth gear and began to pass the Northland Shopping Center on my way out of Lexington. Out of the corner of my left eye I noticed the sign of another Begley's Drug Store, just like the one I had investigated in Shelbyville. I felt it was as good a time as any to buy the substitute lipstick, so I switched on my left-hand signal and pulled into the lot.

Wet as usual (had I ever been dry?), I dripped into the store and began the now well-practiced craning of my neck to determine on which aisle I might find their stock of Bo-Po, Tinkerbell, and so on.

A heavyset woman in her late forties came over to ask if I could be helped. By now a certain similarity of features had begun to emerge in the ladies who worked at the Begley's, Walgreen's, Taylor's and other drug stores. Modified cat's eye glasses dangling from a gold elastic band, heavily rouged cheeks moving rhythmically with the cadence of her chewing gum, her hair coiffed in frozen perfection—this was the lady who stood before me asking, "May I help you?"

"I was looking for play makeup," I said. "Specifically, lipstick."

"We have some in toys," she began, pointing off to a spot at the back of the center aisle. I began ambling back to toys.

"We also used to have some on the hang-up displays over on the specialty racks."

I slowly turned, careful to contain my curiosity. "Did it . . . uh . . . have a little girl on the front . . . and look like a crayon?" I asked, my mouth turning to play-dough.

"Sure did, honey. Let's see, follow me."

Nearly stumbling twice, I followed her to the far side of the store, beginning to babble incoherently about how I had been looking for this certain type of lipstick, but couldn't find it, and if they had any, well, I would be very happy, but I would understand if they didn't, and so on. I'm sure I was saved from being heard, since she had gotten several steps ahead of me and was already thumbing through the pegboard displays when I caught up with her.

"Here we go," she said. I stared in dumbfounded amazement as she went on. "I'm sorry, I don't see the lipstick. I guess we sold out . . . but here's the nail polish . . . in cherry . . . strawberry . . . and here's cologne . . ."

I had never gotten this close before. Like a squirrelly, bearded bookworm who has found a First Edition of *Oliver Twist* on the dollar book shelf, I savored the mere sight of this now antiquated line of children's makeup. There was no lipstick, but perhaps this might be my substitute.

"I'm sorry the lipsticks are gone," she continued, "but we have all of these . . ." she didn't even change her tone of voice, "well, I'll be darned, look what somebody has stuck back here on the wrong hook."

At that moment, the blessing of St. Nicholas descended upon Begley's Drug Store in the Northland Shopping Center, and caused to appear before my very eyes the only unpurchased, fresh, and un-opened package of crayon lipstick like Lindsay Schell's in the Commonwealth of Kentucky. My MasterCard would have been hers for the asking, but it was reduced for clearance to $1.37, and she held it toward me.

"Is this okay?" she asked nonchalantly. I restrained the urge to embrace her on the spot and kiss away the rouge on her cheeks.

"You do not know," I said slowly, trying to keep the lump down in my throat, "how you have helped to make my little girl's Christmas and my own. I'll take it." She smiled passively, not revealing if she knew just what I meant, or was perhaps slightly embarrassed at the Event she had stumbled upon.

I gathered up a modest collection of the remaining makeup and followed her in stunned joy to the check-out counter. I went on to ask her if there were any more lipsticks in the stock room or at another store, and while she was kind enough to check for me, I needn't tell you that I had uncovered the last stick known to mankind.

The rain continued on my way back to Louisville, and neither cleared nor miraculously turned to snow by the time I got back home. I am but a crass human, agent for a greater principal for whom we joyfully toil at this time of year. Yet even I realized on the trip home alone, as I was reminded on Christmas morning when Jennie found her lipstick and held it gleefully upward for all to see, and again whenever I have thought about it since, that a Christmas trust had been fulfilled on aisle one of Begley's Drug Store that rainy December day. It had little to do with play lipstick and everything to do with love, and beyond that, no more need be said.

THE PROMISE KEPT

J oe Solomon made no promises to Ed Davidson before he died.
In fact, once his best friend confided the news of his illness
to Joe, the topic of death was kept from their conversations as one
would avoid acknowledgment of a strand of spinach in someone's
teeth or a stain in their living room carpet. Its reality was ever present
throughout the work day, silently enveloping every conversation, un-
ceasingly dreaded by both, but never discussed. There were no changes
in personnel at the office, no rearrangements of corporate titles, no
new wills drawn. No promises made to visit Ed's mother at Christmas
time.

Joe Solomon reminded himself of all of this as he drove home
from Nashville the weekend before Christmas. Ed had died nearly
five years ago, yet guilt and frustration invaded Joe's being like symp-
toms of a recurrent and immediately recognizable virus. The guilt
was unexplainable. No promises were made. The frustration was that
he should feel guilt at all. Yet they both crept upon him as Joe left
behind the cluster of towers which comprised the new Nashville,
and his car twisted upwards into the last range of Tennessee foothills
worthy of mention. As Joe neared the Kentucky border, he fabricated
one reason after another for not stopping in Gamble, Kentucky to
call upon Ruth Davidson.

Work had resolved all too easily on the Saturday morning of

December 22. The new hospital project was supposed to take the entire weekend. Joe was to return to Louisville on Monday morning. He would pick up Elaine and the children at the airport around noon. She had scheduled a long weekend in Connecticut with her parents to coincide with Joe's efforts in Nashville, but his timetable was undone by a combination of his own success and the impending Christmas holiday. Amidst handshakes and accolades, his presentation had concluded a full day ahead of schedule. That extra day now confined rather than freed Joe Solomon as he drove north.

Five years earlier, another timetable had been undone when nature took a wrong turn and claimed Ed Davidson instead of his seventy-year-old mother. Death had been a contingency entrusted to Ruth Davidson's immediate future, not her son's. That was how Ed had always confided the scenario to Joe and how Ruth had always expected it to run. One day Father Perry, Ruth's parish priest, would phone Ed with the awful news that Ruth had passed away, and Ed would go home to handle the funeral arrangements. It was all planned and prepared. That day never came.

Instead, Joe Solomon had stumbled up the steep hill of the cemetery with Ruth Davidson on his arm, stood around the neatly bordered family plot, remembered none of the prayers or final words which Father Perry spoke, and said good-bye to his friend. Joe retained a vivid memory of the wind which whistled through leafless trees overhead and the trek back down the hill with Ruth Davidson. She implored Joe to visit her some time, he nodded noncommittally and slipped out of Gamble, Kentucky. No promises were made.

Joe's reflection on the past ended with the sign ahead: "Welcome to Kentucky, the Bluegrass State." The sun, which had been a constant irritant to him as he drove into the Tennessee hills, now crept below the last rise of Kentucky farmland. Night quickly consumed the road, and erased the last of the countryside diversions. The town of Gamble was only twenty miles further north. If Joe was going to formulate a good excuse for not visiting Ruth Davidson this Christmas, he needed more time to collect his thoughts. A memory had become a guilt-plagued thought, the thought had evolved into an obsession, and the obsession would surely blossom into uncontrolled action if he stayed on the highway.

Releasing some of the pressure on the gas pedal, Joe slowed to the legal speed limit, eased into the right hand lane and pulled off of the expressway at Brighton, Kentucky. Ahead of him loomed a tower-like sign for Trucker's Rest, and Joe decided that a cup of coffee might give him the time he needed. Once off the road, he might be able to weigh the impact of a visit to Ruth Davidson and the possible commitments he might unwittingly make or the sadnesses he might unknowingly inflict. A cup of coffee would be just the thing.

Joe walked into the Trucker's Rest and stopped for a second while his pupils, recently opened wide to adjust to the night, narrowed to allow for the piercing fluorescence. He gathered his balance and walked past rows of country knickknacks, country candy, and country wood-crafts to the decidedly urban cafe counter, where he joined two drivers who were discussing the remainder of their journey to Cleveland. He sat down on the outskirts of the wreckage created by their black coffee and Marlboros.

The counter waitress was enthralled by the truckers' tales of high-way adventures, and with considerable difficulty she disengaged her-self long enough to take Joe's order. She labored over her thick pad of thin order sheets and half glanced at Joe as she asked without emotion, "What can I get for you?"

"Just a cup of coffee, and a piece of that Dutch Apple pie . . . that piece would be just fine," Joe pointed to one of the two last wedges of pastry beneath the glass dome on the counter, "and cream . . . lots of cream."

She slid the pie from beneath its cover and onto a plate. Then she poured a mug of coffee with surprising panache and placed mug, pie plate, and bill in front of Joe.

"Thanks."

"You're welcome." She smiled for the first time.

"And Merry Christmas," Joe ventured.

She smiled again. "I'm working Christmas Eve. Wouldn't you know it."

The waitress moved down the counter, and Joe tested the first bite of pie. It was hardly fresh-baked and only recently thawed, but it was sweet and filling, and Joe finished it quickly. He blew the steam from his coffee and stared unseeingly at the front wall of the cafe.

Without purpose or order, memories of a similar setting began to overcome the emptiness of his thoughts. The time was nearly thirty years past, and he sat, one week before Christmas, with his mother at the soda fountain of the long-departed Newberry's Dime Store in downtown Cincinnati. A shopping bag at his side held socks for his father, a gold-filled locket for his sister, a scarf for his grandmother, and a pair of gloves for his grandfather. He had bought them all within his budget. Joe's mother topped her coffee cup with cream and con-gratulated Joe on his good work. Then she took a sip of coffee and carefully set the cup down.

"What do you want, Mommy?" Joe asked.

"Your love and whatever you want to give me. If I give you any hints, I won't be surprised."

"I guess you're right," Joe conceded. He remembered the little porcelain figure of a choir boy which his mother had noted just moments before in the window of a music store. With the iron resolution of a nine-year-old, Joe determined to return to downtown with another adult before the week was over. The choir boy would be a perfect gift. The nine-year-old Joe emptied the last of his vanilla malt from the stainless steel mixing canister, then looked at his mother.

"I really liked the movie. Especially the chariot race and the part where Ben-Hur finds his sister and mother. Can we go to the movies again, soon?"

"Well, of course, Joe. The older you get, the more we can go. That's a promise."

It was a promise Joe's mother wasn't able to keep. She died suddenly one evening the following spring. Joe had managed to return to downtown Cincinnati to buy the porcelain choir boy, and she had confided to him that it was her favorite Christmas gift.

"Need a refill, mister?" The girl behind the counter jolted him into the present.

"Uh, yes, just a little. Not much . . . that's fine," Joe stumbled.

Thirty years after his Newberry's malted milk, Joe Solomon realized with blazing clarity that his avoidance of Ruth Davidson was rooted in more than the death of his best friend. Ed should be going home to Ruth or Joe should be going home to his own mother, but the mismatch which seemed to be moving ever closer to reality was neither fair nor redeeming. Yet the meeting was forthcoming. Joe knew that now, just as certainly as he had known that he would buy that porcelain choir boy.

In that moment between his last sip of coffee and the payment of his bill, Joe felt more ill at ease having resolved that he would stop in Gamble than he had during the debate over whether he should. A definite thought and purpose were no comfort. It was like the dream he sometimes had of walking into a meeting of his business associates with no clothes on. It started sensibly enough, but the realization during his dream of just what he had done sent him desperately searching for cover. In a short while, he would be walking out of his dream of the past five years, confronting Ruth Davidson with the nakedness of his guilt and sorrow. It was frightening, inevitable, and above all, real.

The moon had risen higher by the time Joe returned to the expressway. One by one, he counted the eighteen mile markers between Brighton and Gamble. Joe took the Gamble exit and turned left for the business district. He remembered the way to Ed's house fairly well, but a few landmarks had come down, and a few gas stations had cropped up in their place. He went forward slowly, cautiously, but with no doubt that within a few minutes he would be face to face with his best friend's mother.

Toward the center of town he saw a phone booth and wondered for a moment whether he should call her first. No, he thought, because Ruth Davidson might decline or she might not be at home, and in either event, he would then be unable to stand on his dead friend's front porch and knock upon his dead friend's front door. Both were things, he realized, he now needed to do.

So he passed the phone booth, and another shortly after it, wound around the courthouse, and started back out of the business district. Past the Gamble County Bank, he turned left. Past Ed's old high school and past Ed's parish church and past Ed's first girl friend's house and past the old buckeye tree where Ed and the neighborhood kids had fought for possession of the most buckeyes. Past the nondescript corner where two fraternity brothers had commiserated over lost loves and become fast friends one spring night. Little had changed.

Joe made one more left turn and coasted along the row of two-story white houses which led to the Davidsons' home. Then, before he was prepared, as if he would ever be prepared, he arrived at Ed's house. For Joe, five years were erased in the passage of a moment. Slightly shabbier than the other homes, its peeling paint more noticeable, its drooping gutters more pronounced, Ed's house stood gloriously whole. Though weatherworn, the house had survived.

Joe got out of his car and stared at the house. From his vantage point on the street, it seemed to be winking at him. One second-floor gable was lit—Ruth's room. One second-floor gable was unlit—Ed's room. From the front parlor, through a long window with small, tooth-like panes, shone a soft light which gave the house the appearance of a smile. It seemed to welcome him.

The wind of a newly formed cold front began to pick up in force, tearing at Joe's cheeks and cutting through his overcoat as he moved toward the house. The brick front walk seemed to extend without end. Three steps led to a front door which had not seen paint for five years. Joe brought the bar of the door knocker down softly, and heard nothing. He repeated the motion twice, more loudly, and heard the muffled sounds of someone moving inside.

The door opened, and the soft light he had noticed from the street spread over him like a blanket. Ruth Davidson stood before him, her left hand still on the door knob, her right hand clutching the top of her cardigan to her neck. She stared at Joe, then cocked her head slightly and stepped back. A look of astonishment crept into her features, then a slow, warm smile, and Ruth Davidson's eyes spoke before her lips formed words. Joe read her eyes and stepped in, closing the door gently behind him.

"You've come . . . at last . . ." she said quietly. Then she turned to her right, leading Joe further into the room. Joe followed her and found himself, in silence, standing in the middle of a parlor that had not changed in five years.

An unadorned Christmas tree, fresh and tall, stood in the corner next to the window and the fireplace. By the fireplace, an old-fashioned, four-foot tall, plastic Santa Claus seemed poised to fly up the chimney. Stacks of ancient boxes, obviously filled to overflowing with lights and ornaments, were situated on the opposite side of the fireplace. On the mantelpiece, lined up like so many toy soldiers, were photos of Ed Davidson on Santa's lap, framed in department store cardboard, and yellowed with age.

Joe Solomon's frustration, guilt, and fear dissolved and were replaced in an instant with the irrepressible urge to cry for the loss of his friend. He somehow held it back, tried to find a word or two, and failed. Ruth Davidson leaned over carefully, took the cord from the Santa Claus, and plugged it in. She turned, and Joe saw for the first time a wandering look in her eye which matched the slightly disheveled waves in her hair and the faintly observable wrinkles in her dress.

"You've come home for Christmas, Ed," she said simply. "I knew you would. I have missed you so much." Before Joe could register shock or deny her words, she had moved into his arms and held him tightly with a mother's grip.

Five years had passed quickly for Joe Solomon. For Ruth, the past five years had taken her into her seventies and slowly out of reality. In Gamble, everyone knew Ruth Davidson had grown a bit "touched" with encroaching age. The formal name for it came up on the television or in the papers every now and then, but they tended not to use it. They simply understood that Ruth's world was often different from that of other folks.

Now she stood clutching her boy for a small eternity, and Joe Solomon held her in return, confused and overcome. Her embrace slowly loosened, and she removed herself slightly, enough to look with her dreaming eyes into Joe's face.

"Can you stay long enough to decorate the tree?" The faintest glimmer of true understanding passed like a shadow over her face. "I know you have to leave soon. But maybe you could go with me to Mass tomorrow morning?"

Joe Solomon's own grasp on reality began to fade as his eyes darted from Ruth to the stacks of boxed ornaments. He sensed that, once revealed, the ornaments would be identical to those which his own mother had collected through the forties and fifties. Time had made known to him one of its odd little wrinkles. There was no other place that he should be and no other person with whom he should be. He looked around again as if to confirm there were no other eyes watching. Except for Ed's childhood Christmas photos lined up on the mantle, they were alone. Joe's family was far away, the town of Gamble was settling down for the night, and the memories of Ed were alive. Joe hesitated for a millisecond, uncertain whether he should dissolve her delusion, unsettled as to his own emotions. Then he caught his breath, and in the fulfillment of promises made but unspoken, stepped into the role that each wanted so badly.

"Of course," he said simply. "You know I will."

Joe asked no questions and offered no answers. With his simple statement, Joe felt the joy of a mother's love overtake him as he imparted to Ruth Davidson the love of a long-awaited son.

"Well, let's start with the lights first . . . you remember, from the top down." With those simple words of direction, Ruth reached into a box, removed an old strand of large-bulbed lights, and placed them in Joe's hand.

They began the decoration of the tree, speaking seldom, and then only in short, hushed sentences, as if they were in church. From lights they progressed to ornaments—large on the bottom and small near the top; the more valued glass balls where they could be seen, the less valued foil and paper creations around toward the corner. At last, they wrapped up their work in gold strands of furry tinsel. When the last box was empty, and the ceremony done, they admired their work together.

"Well," Joe said at last, "it's getting late. I'd better get my things." Joe gathered his belongings from the car and went to Ed's room. Ruth turned off the light in the hall and retired.

When the morning came, they ate breakfast and spoke of old friends and old times. Though Ruth often repeated her stories, or ended them in the middle, trailing off with giggles of delight, Joe made sense of it. Nothing more mattered. They cleared away the breakfast dishes and dressed for church, completing a Sunday ritual which Joe performed as if it were his own.

Into the light of day and before the eyes of the congregation, Joe accompanied Ruth to church. As he had escorted her from Ed's last resting place, Joe helped Ruth to her pew, conscious of the friendly eyes about him, but secure in the knowledge that his secret was preserved.

When the service was over, and as Ruth's friends were wishing them well, Father Perry made a point of finding Joe outside the church. He held out his hand, then drew Joe toward him.

"Thanks for coming, Joe," he whispered. "I helped Ruth bring the tree in last night. She knew you'd be coming. She told me, 'he's coming home tonight, Father,' and God bless me, she was right. Come back soon."

Joe shook Father Perry's hand again, and with the sense that a covenant had been completed, smiled at the priest.

"I will, Father. You can bet on it," Joe said softly. "That's a promise."

BENEFIT OF THE BARGAIN

Along, high-pitched wail from the rail yards sounded the passage of the Chesapeake and Ohio freight on its way from Louisville to Lexington. It was December 20, the last school day before Christmas. Janet Law (Miss Law to her fifth graders) looked at the old, brown school clock which hung over the oval portrait of George Washington to confirm that it was three o'clock. Her own fifth grade room in Birmingham had had such a perfectly accurate, consummately nondescript clock, which ceased to run only upon the occasion when Franklin Hawley knocked it off the wall with a rubberized baseball. When it was safely placed back upon the wall, and Franklin placed in the principal's office, it resumed its watch upon her young life.

Tapping her red pencil on the edge of her desk, Janet glanced from the clock to the timeless, gray December day outside of her long bank of windows. The playground was empty. If it weren't for the last-minute semester grades and the problem of David Mays, she would be with Susan and Lucy having a glass of wine at the little inn just outside the county line. "Oh, well," Janet thought, brushing her newly cropped brown hair, "another day, another dollar."

Janet fully intended to continue grading the spelling test in front of her, but thoughts of childhood, begun by looking at the clock, continued as the colored rings of construction paper, tin foil stars, and strings of popcorn and berries which adorned the tree reminded her of Christmases past. She was lost in thoughts of another decade when her classroom door suddenly flung open.

Janet started, knocking her purse from the edge of her desk. She picked up the purse and composed herself while David Mays stood in her doorway, waiting for his punishment. Taller than his ten-year-old peers, and only an inch shorter than Janet, more outspoken than even the sixth graders one year older, and black and proud as any student she had ever taught, David had somehow become her special charge.

"Janet . . ." The principal had stopped her during the lunch break. His voice lowered to a whisper. "David Mays called Miss Christian an old white bitch in the hall this morning."

"Well?" she had answered, knowing full well what was next. She liked Bob Jones as a person, but avoided him as a principal.

"Well, I've got a conference with the superintendent this afternoon. And then, well," he stammered, "I'm supposed to pick up Betty and the kids and go into Louisville to shop right after school. And you've got more control over David than anyone else has. Why, for you he would . . ."

"Okay, Mr. Jones. When, how, and just what am I supposed to do?"

"Well, I've told him to report to you after school. You can . . . well, do something . . . you know . . . do something." He patted her on the shoulder and smiled anemically, moving quickly on through the corridor. He had known she would stay, even on the last day before vacation.

"Hello, David," she said, regaining her teacher's tone of voice. "Have a seat." He began to sit down. "Up here, by me, where I don't have to scream unless I want to." Janet smiled. David moved to the seat by the side of her desk.

Janet was not completely prepared for the moment. In fact, she had no details of the offense. And she certainly had no idea of the sentence she was to administer.

"David, let's get to the point," she said. "Mr. Jones says you called Miss Christian an old white bitch." She was careful not to stumble over or slur the phrase "old white bitch." "What do you have to say about that?"

David pursed his lips and looked down at his lap. A few seconds passed and he looked up.

"Well, David, why?"

"Because she talked bad to me."

"What did she say?" Janet asked, knowing that the confession would not flow easily.

"She said I was stealing." Janet guessed that this was not a direct quote.

"Why would she have thought you were stealing?"

"Cause of the money I took. But I told her I was going to pay it back."

"Whom did you take the money from?"

"Brian." Brian was white, and ordinarily David's closest friend.

"Was it just Brian whom you took money from?" Janet's mind wandered for a moment to the grammatical offense of ending her sentence with a preposition.

"Well, there was Tom and Craig, too . . . I would have paid them back. I would have paid them all back. I was just borrowing."

"So it was their money?"

"Yes . . . but I needed it. I need it now. So I took it. But I told them I'd pay them back. They knew."

Janet knew David was loud, and boastful, competitive, and proud. He was not dishonest.

"What was the money for, David?"

"Things," David answered. His jaws set tightly. Janet knew she would get no further response with a direct question.

The room became silent except for the recurring squeak of David's sneaker on the linoleum floor. The gray overcast outside had begun to deepen as it neared 3:30. A few premature flakes of snow began to settle down from the gray, dusting the black limbs of the oak tree outside Janet's window. Crime and punishment were the last topics Janet wanted to pursue.

Even without this last bit of "housekeeping," it was not the merriest of Christmases. Almost one year after her divorce, Janet had no one who even vaguely resembled a "significant other." She had resolved that since Louisville was home now, she would not flee back to Birmingham for Christmas. When all was said and done, wine with Susan and Lucy was more to the order of her emotional tolerance than what lay before her now.

"What are you doing for Christmas, David?" If David didn't want to talk about petty theft then neither did she, at least for the moment.

"Stayin' with Momma." Janet knew that this meant with his mother and his stepfather.

"Have you trimmed your tree yet?"

"They did." Janet knew that this meant his mother, stepfather, and their children.

"Didn't you help?" Janet probed.

"I had chores. Jim said I'm getting too old for trimming trees and Santa Claus and all that."

Janet's breath escaped in a short, quiet hiss. At twenty-nine, she too sensed the need for trimming trees and Santa Claus. Her parents *had* asked her to join them and her teenage brother. A gut feeling midway between pride and shame had prompted her to decline the offer. David lacked the good fortune of an offer. Janet collected her thoughts, then herself.

"What about your Daddy's family?" David's natural father had been killed in an industrial accident four years before. Somehow the lawyer Mrs. Mays had retained managed to lose the worker's compensation case, failing to file before the two year deadline. David's stepfather was a good man, but a hard one.

"They're away."

"Who's away?"

"Aunt Jane's moved to St. Louis. Uncle Fred's family are all busy." David fell silent, resuming his gaze downward at his squeaking sneaker. At last, Janet had a lead and a clue. David had not mentioned his grandmother Mays.

"When is your Grandmother Mays coming to town for Christmas?"

David simply shook his head from side to side.

"Where does she live, David?"

"Cincinnati."

"Do you think your stepdad doesn't have the money for her busfare down here?" Janet was guessing.

"Jim says so. He got laid off Friday. Plant's closing till February."

"So you were trying to get the money from Brian, Tom, and Craig so you could pay for a ticket, right?"

David's eyes darted upwards with a look of respect for her intelligence and resentment for her intrusion into his sadness.

"Yeah . . ." he started. "And it would have been okay. They knew I'd pay 'em back. But they saw Miss Christian and got scared. And then when she stopped us they wouldn't say anything."

The mention of Miss Christian added yet another wrinkle to the problem. Janet was suddenly reminded that Miss Christian had been called "an old white bitch," and was probably waiting for an outcome to the incident in her own room. Ethel Christian was both strict and kind, tough-minded and sensitive, and above all, if Janet were David's mother figure at the school, Ethel Christian was his surrogate grandmother.

Janet looked down at the clutter on her unvarnished desk top. She could use some order and a little time to think. She knew that she had neither. Getting up from her desk, Janet walked to the window. What a strange little episode to arise so perilously close to Christmas. It threatened all three of them at once. And if the spirit of the holiday had seemed merely distant earlier in the day, it now seemed utterly beyond reach.

The money was the least of Janet's problems. Janet Law had little to spare, but certainly enough to pay for a bus ticket from Cincinnati. The question was how to find a solution that constituted punishment rather than reward. She turned and looked at David, still seated by her desk. Punishment would get her nowhere. Charity would not get her that far.

"David," she began, thinking as her words were spoken. "Your punishment is that you must bargain with me. Ordinarily you would have the choice not to. But I am the teacher and you are the student and because of what you said to Miss Christian, I am taking that choice from you." David began to stiffen. He did not like being told that any of his choices had been eliminated, and even if he did not fully realize what Janet had in mind, he understood well enough to feel angry. She understood too, and was relieved. Now she could proceed.

"I will now present the terms of our bargain."

"What kind of bargain?" David snapped.

"I will trade you the price of a round trip bus ticket for your Grandmother Mays for certain . . ." She paused. "Certain work."

"What kind of work?" His voice softened a little.

"You tell me what you'll be willing to do and I'll tell you whether I'll accept. But it must also involve Miss Christian."

David's chin receded and his back assumed a more normal slope. "I'll apologize," David mumbled.

"That's to be expected, David. That's only common decency."

He paused, confused. "I'll mean it," he finally said quietly.

"That's a beginning." Janet smiled slightly. "And what else will you do?"

David looked down and away. "I'll be good."

"Now you're back to square one. You are 'good,' David. That's not the issue." She knew that when David looked down and away his mind was not on his words.

"You must offer me something that I will accept and that I believe you'll come through on." Janet bit her lip as she repeated her grammatical error. She brushed the intruding thought aside.

David looked up and squarely into her eyes. "What can I do?" he asked.

"That's something you need to decide," Janet answered.

He glanced outside at the dense gray cloud cover. "I'd shovel snow, but I don't have no shovel."

"I don't have *any* shovel," Janet corrected him. She caught herself in the pedant's bind and quickly added, "I accept your offer. It's a deal." She calculated that Susan and Lucy were on their second glass of wine by now.

"What? But . . ."

"I know, David. No shovel. I'll worry about the details later—just come with me." She rose from her chair, took David by the hand, and quickly marched down the length of the second-floor corridor, their footfalls echoing against the twelve-foot ceilings and beige walls. They reached their destination at the end of the hall and waited for a moment in silence.

Miss Christian sat waiting at her desk, gazing out the window, her hands folded over her gloves, her purse ready for departure. Janet knocked at the half-open door.

"Excuse me, Miss Christian. David Mays and I would like to see you for a moment. David has something he would like to say to you."

She stepped into the room, dropped David's hand from hers, and took one step back to the door. Miss Christian looked steadily into David's eyes. Janet diverted her own gaze to the brown clock on Miss Christian's wall and achingly watched the sweep hand make its way from one to almost seven before she dared look back at the two actors in the drama unfolding before her. Ethel's eyes reflected the hurt suffered earlier in the day, and the muscles of her jaw seemed to be tense with the effort of holding back anger or tears or both.

Six years in the school system had gradually taught Janet the folklore that surrounded Ethel Christian. She had cast her first vote in a national election for Franklin Roosevelt the year after she began teaching. Nearly thirty years later she voted for John Kennedy at the 1960 convention, and openly cried and closed her classroom the day Norman Williams came running in with the news that the president was dead. She voted for Carter secretly in 1976 and more secretly in 1980, only after still more secretly voting for another Kennedy brother in the Democratic primary.

Her attempts at concealment were futile. It was a small-town school and the small town had pegged her as a liberal. Ethel Christian had remained in her classroom at Northside Elementary when it integrated in 1958, lived through phone calls in the night, and survived cries of "nigger lover" when she shielded a first-grade student from rotten eggs. She was also getting old, and words like "old white bitch" cut easily through the stern facade she had cultivated over a fifty-year tenure. She would retire in June at age seventy-two.

David raised his head. His large, deep brown eyes never blinked.

"Miss Christian, I'm sorry. I'm awfully sorry. I said something that wasn't me. I like you. My family likes you. But you remind me of my Grandma. And *she* wasn't going to be here this Christmas.

And I was trying to get money to pay her way. And I was mad. Brian and Tom and Craig knew. But they was scared. And you were the only one stopping me." He stopped for breath, his words rushing closer together. "I'll shovel your walk when the snow comes. This winter and every winter. Not just 'cause Miss Law will pay me . . ." he paused, unsure if the bargain was private or not, "but cause I want to. You've done good by me and my family and they all know it and you don't have nobody and I don't . . ." David was crying. Ethel Christian stepped forward, holding her breath, the dam that was holding back her tears about to break. She put her arms around David's shoulders and he wrapped his gangly arms about her torso.

They stood in the silence shared only with Janet and the bare, gray country playground outside. Janet felt a tear forming and the need to leave the scene without breaking it. She slipped back, then out the door, catching and preserving for a later day the brief glance of gratitude and peace in Miss Christian's eye.

Janet walked the hallway alone this time, quickly took her one crisp twenty-dollar bill from her wallet, placed it in an envelope, and rapidly scribbled on the outside: "David Mays. For services performed and to be rendered."

She returned to Miss Christian's room in the growing darkness. Their embrace broken, teacher and student stood side by side, David's right arm about her broad back, her left propped lightly on his shoulders, staring out the window at two squirrels running up and down the limbs which crisscrossed and rubbed against the windows of the school.

"I need to get going," Janet said. Her voice had become husky. They turned around. Miss Christian came to her and David followed.

"Thank you, Janet. You have been a capable mediator in our little dispute." Even while Ethel Christian verbally resumed the persona of Teacher that she had chiseled upon herself for fifty years, the gentle squeeze Janet felt on her hand related much more. "Please have a very merry Christmas. And do have a good visit with your family. They must love you very much."

Janet hesitated, then smiled politely. Poor Ethel Christian. Perhaps she was slipping. Janet had mentioned over lunch just the other day that she would not be staying with her parents over Christmas.

"David," Janet said, handing him the envelope, "here's the benefit of our bargain. It looks like we have all been well served." David hugged her, harder, tighter, like he would have hugged his mother. He looked up and said nothing.

A sudden change of expression flashed over David's face. Janet read his thoughts.

"The shovel," Janet said. "I almost forgot. Miss Christian, David needs a shovel. Do you have one he can borrow?"

"Of course."

"Good. You two work out the rental," she joked. "Now I've got to run."

The corridor was now immersed in dull shadows, making nearly indiscernible the walls covered with the first-graders' Christmas trees and Santa Claus scenes. Janet hurried to her room, grabbed her purse, gathered her books, shuffled together thirty-six book reports, slipped into her coat, and wrapped her scarf around her neck twice. Then for a moment she paused, caught in the last gray hours of an endless gray day. The school room itself seemed even lonelier than her. Its charges were gone for the holidays, its mistress was about to leave. And it would stand ready and eager and yearning for the noise, the coughs, the shuffling feet, the trash paper, and the scrapes and bruises to be brought within its walls after the new year. Janet thrust her arm into the strap of her purse, picked up her briefcase, and left the room behind her for the holidays.

The rush of cold air first took her breath away, then invigorated her as Janet crossed the gravel parking lot and fumbled with the stiff door lock of her Chevette. The car turned over on the fourth try and Janet sat shivering while she waited for the heater to kick in. Loosening the brake and sputtering slowly forward, she eased past the school just as David Mays emerged from the front door. Slipping into second gear, she honked the horn in a moment of farewell and celebration. Past the county library and Murphy's Furniture store on her right, past the Winn-Dixie and Rexall Drug Store on her left. Janet was warm, in fifth gear, and going fifty when she left the city limits headed for Louisville.

Two hundred yards ahead, Susan and Lucy's cars stood out clearly in the parking lot of the Old Stone Inn. Janet slowed to third gear and put on her right signal light. For a moment she contemplated the method by which she would share her afternoon with Susan and Lucy, then realized she simply couldn't. It was too fragile out of context, and when they left the last sip of wine in their glasses and returned to Louisville for an evening with family or friends, Janet would leave for her apartment and the breakfast dishes.

It was probably the dirty dishes that decided the issue. Janet turned off her signal, shifted back into fourth gear, and turned at the next ramp onto the expressway. Turning on the radio, Janet adjusted her seat slightly backward for a longer trip. Without even thinking twice about stopping for clothes (her mother, like her, was a perfect four), Janet wound around the city on the Watterson Expressway, then turned south for Birmingham. The towns rolled by like depot stops on an old fashioned train route: Elizabethtown, Cave City, Bowling Green, Franklin, Nashville and south.

She got off the expressway at the Murfreesboro "midway" point and was halfway through a Wendy's single with cheese when a discordant thought made her sit upright. All the way down I-65 and halfway through dinner she had been wondering whether *David* would benefit from his experience; she had reviewed the afternoon's events and wondered whether his grandmother would come, whether he would keep his contract and whether he would ultimately learn and profit from her solution. Then she remembered that Ethel Christian had wished *her* a good visit with her family. Had Miss Christian really forgotten, or did she know more than Janet the full consideration Janet had received from her contract with David?

The rain outside was turning to sleet and Janet rebuttoned her coat and took the remainder of her coffee with her, eager to move on toward Birmingham. She wondered then, and would wonder again when Ethel Christian retired and David Mays moved on to Middle School the next year, whether, after all, she had received the greatest benefit of the bargain struck that lonely afternoon.

REMEMBER THE
ORANGES

R emember the oranges." Those were her last words.
Four days before Christmas I had started out for Martin's
Toy Store with a list tucked into my pocket and every intention of
filling it. Then I strayed; something had triggered my melancholy. I
had taken an intentional wrong turn, then another, and found myself
in the cemetery. Leaning against my car door, I stared at my grandmother's grave. It should have shown signs from the funeral just one
week before, but it was as smooth and unmarred as if it had been
there for decades. Today's gravediggers knew their trade.

Thanksgiving, just four weeks before, seemed like a day out of
another life. Only on reflection had Grandma seemed thinner, more
frail, perhaps less talkative. We spoke that night about gift lists, church
caroling, potluck dinners, and the annual pageant. The family was
together. The kids were only passingly destructive; no permanent dam-
age was done to person or property. We were traveling gently in the
mid-current of life, ignorant of any eddies ahead.

The week after Thanksgiving, the call came to my office.

"You'd better get to the hospital, Jeb." My grandmother's neighbor,
Mrs. Wobbly, had a way of pausing after statements like that. It was
her self-annointed duty in life to intermingle suspense, fear, and a

hint of guilt in any of her conversations with me that concerned Grandma. I refused to wait for her next studied and forlorn breath.

"Well, what is it? Has Grandma had an accident?"

"She called me this morning, Jeb. I don't think she wanted to bother you." Mrs. Wobbly evoked guilt with the style of a master. Grandma would have loved it. "She fainted in the bathroom. The ambulance left about five minutes ago."

I calmly thanked Mrs. Wobbly. Despite her conscience-of-the-world tone, she was a good neighbor and one of a handful of my grandmother's remaining friends.

There was nothing calm about my trip to the hospital. I ran two red lights and drove the wrong way into the parking garage. By the time I was directed to the correct room, Grandma had been given something to make her sleep. I stood at the foot of her bed dreading the worst, slipping into a world of sickness and death that for me had been nonexistent just an hour before. In the days to come, the routine of the hospital would become the norm and the Christmas preparations of the rest of humanity foreign.

"Your grandmother's a very sick woman." Grandma's family physician, Dr. Lake, had been waiting for me at the nurse's station. His voice dropped, then trailed off into a Mrs. Wobbly pause. I could have grabbed him by the lapels of his tweed coat.

"Well?" I insisted.

"I don't know how she could have gone on this long. She has a very large uterine tumor. It's cut off her bladder function . . . basically set off a bout of uremic poisoning."

"So can you operate?"

"No . . . we really can't. She'd never survive. We could never separate it out. It's just a matter of a few days . . . a couple of weeks at most."

He said more, but it was lost in a low hum that had begun in my ears, then seemed to fill my entire head. The grey-green, institutional hall, the comfortable disarray of the nurses' station, and the polite monotone of Dr. Lake all grew distant. I strained to record and mentally repeat each word, but, even as I did, all of his words blurred together.

As I stood in the cemetery on the day of winter solstice three weeks later, every nuance of light and sound and smell would leap back to be vividly relived. But standing outside of her hospital room, being told that a very definite end awaited our love and friendship, it was more like the beginning of a horrific dream. I would have given anything to wake up, but I knew instead that I would plod through to the end. This dream could have only one resolution. There would be no sigh of relief in the darkness of four A.M., no euphoria at the grant of another chance to dream a different dream.

The topic of death had never been taboo between Grandma and me. We had more than touched on its inevitability. We had even reminisced on its sting—taking my mother when I was young and my father when I was in college. We had often wondered by what design we were left alone of the family to sputter forward with our little segment of the race.

"Jeb," my Grandma had said, "if I lead a good life . . . and I'm kind to others . . . treat them as I would have them treat me . . . do you think God will take me quickly?"

The thought of God ever taking her was an initial shock, but I had eased into the mood of the conversation.

"I don't think He dispenses those kinds of favors," I had observed sagely.

"That's what I was afraid you'd say." She giggled like the little girl she had always been. "Well, let's see if we can't put it off a while longer, anyway. I want to know your children a little better first."

We had talked about so much through the years—growing up, love, marriage, love-making, children, world politics, funny stories from the turn of the century, funny stories from yesterday's trip to the grocery.

"Jeb, did I ever tell you about the day your grandfather drove the Packard through the front window of Al Noble's gas station?" She hadn't, and we both laughed until she could barely sit up straight and my sides cramped.

"Bless his heart, he had Al fix the window and swear he'd never tell me . . . and Al didn't. It was Sam Voigt, the druggist. He had seen the whole thing. And even he kept it to himself until your grandfather was dead. Then he got tickled one day talking to me, and he just had to tell me all about it." She had paused and sipped her coffee, looking out the back window.

"I wonder, Jeb, what it will be like to be joined again with your mother and your grandfather. I can't say it won't be nice . . . if that's what heaven's all about . . . but I'll miss you."

We had been lucky for those times over coffee and breakfast, or when I dropped by in the evenings. During her two weeks in the hospital, reality was neither warm nor memorable. Reality was slipping in and out of the hospital's parking garage at all hours of the day and night. Trying to catch Grandma when the drugs were just wearing off, when we might relish a second or two of thought or feeling before pain forced the next dose of morphine and the end of our time together worth noting. And during those two weeks, it seemed to me as if everyone around me was skipping gleefully and obliviously on their way toward filling Christmas gift lists.

"Look," my wife approached me with the care accorded a wounded animal, "I want you to go to the hospital as much as you want to, but the children are beginning to miss you as much as they miss Grandma. They think you're sick, too. It's all beginning to get confused in their minds."

My fist started swiftly towards the kitchen table, but I curbed its path into my palm.

"You're right . . . this is crazy. I get home or go to the office, and I fidget until I can get back to the hospital. I get to the hospital and Grandma's asleep and they tell me she's been calling for me. Then I feel awful. If I ask them to hold up on the painkillers until I get there, I feel worse. If they follow their standing orders, then I miss the few seconds that would mean anything. And once I'm there . . . I sit for five minutes . . . I start fidgeting . . . and I can't wait to get out of there . . ." I droned on, my words transforming into a repetitive drivel.

Susan listened with more patience than I probably deserved. I paused and she tried to ease me back onto the subject of gifts.

"Do you want me to do the kids' Christmas shopping?"

"No . . . no, I'll do it." My reaction was stubborn and inescapable. I always did it. That was the important part of Christmas for me. Giving had long since replaced the joy of receiving.

Our disjointed conversation ended. I put on my coat and returned to the hospital.

"Remember the oranges." My grandmother's last shopping list had come from her lips with the tinkling gaiety of wind chimes. She smiled, her eyes glistened, as if fully cognizant of all that was happening, then she slipped into her final coma. I had stayed by her side, grasping her hand, whispering embarrassed little phrases of encouragement. Two hours had passed, her grip tightened, her eyelids fluttered, and she had died.

The nurses were all very kind. They expected no hysterics, and I displayed none. Grandma was eighty-four. Old folks died every day. Even at Christmas time. I was thirty-four—old enough to cope maturely with the loss of a grandparent.

Only a few of them knew that I was Grandma's only grandson, she my only surviving link with childhood family. Even before my mother's death, we had shared a communion of souls—we were born on the same birthday, fifty years apart. When I cried, I made sure they didn't see me.

And what were her last words to me? What solace did I have that evening as I left the hospital to tell my children that their great-grandmother wouldn't be with them this Christmas? "Remember the oranges." I almost wished she had added, ". . . and the apples. And don't forget a head of lettuce and a half pound of sliced turkey." Shopping. Part of the daily ritual, the ceremony of seeing her friends, stocking the refrigerator and pantry, underscoring her independence by driving her car all over town, seeing the town and being seen. These things were important. And if her grocery list was important to her in her final delirious moments of waking, then it was important to me as well. Yet I wanted more. I wanted epiphany, some final passage to close out our thirty-four years of friendship. A week later, standing mute in the fading afternoon, I was no closer to finding it.

The wind died down, and the flurries I was sure would cease had begun to powder the ground. I reached inside of my coat pocket. The scribbled sheet of note paper was there where Susan had tucked it before I left the house. I glanced at it beneath the soft pink hue of reflected city lights.

"Barbie outfits, Barbie kitchen, Barbie bath . . ." I could clean out one aisle and be halfway done. "Legos, jet commandos, radio-controlled car . . ." Not as easy, but not too difficult, either. I smiled. There had been no need for the list; I knew it by heart. But Susan had foreseen my distraction. She might as well have drawn a map to Martin's Toys. Her list was simply a reminder.

More like a maze than a simple way out, the road out of the cemetery seemed to make more false turns than true. The last gate was ready to close when I finally escaped its grounds. The guard looked relieved as I left. Cars packed with shoppers streamed past me on the main artery out of the city. I turned up the radio and joined them. It felt good to be among the living.

"Okay," I thought, "no more distractions along the way."

The ordinary provided comfort. Like everyone else who has ever decried the gross materialism of Christmas, I quickly slipped into cherishing my thoughts of it. Like Americans of good cheer throughout the country, I hoped that Barbie and G.I. Joe would convey some ethereal message of love. So what if Barbie was a miniature out of a grown man's fantasy and G.I. Joe a purveyor of Pentagon propaganda? The harm was negligible. So, probably, was my rationale. But I was happy to be on my way.

The shopping strip's alternative to an evangelical church's lighted cross loomed before me. The three-story, neon clown sparkled in the light snowfall, announcing the proximity of Martin's Toys. I circled the parking lot twice, then landed a prime spot on the third swing around. Now I was on a roll, focused and ready to buy.

The huge glass sliding doors shot back as I approached them. Even the electric eye seemed happy to see me stumbling into the swing of things.

I grabbed a shopping cart and started for the location where experience had taught me that Barbie had her hideout. Easy-listening Christmas carols seemed to seep syrup-like from every wall and ceiling panel, never enough to distract, but just enough to lull someone into the mood. Then the melody stopped, and the cacophonous rattle of my broken shopping cart resounded on the hard tile floor.

When the music started again it was real music. Some errant soul at the manager's station in front had decided to vary the program. Before I knew it, Bing Crosby was singing "I'll Be Home for Christmas."

Seconds before I had been anesthetized by manufactured easy-listening. Now feelings overwhelmed me. Sharply detailed memories merged with vague recollections of a past Christmas or past Christmases. I could see my grandmother teetering near the top of an eight-foot ladder, unsafe from its first step upwards.

"Okay, Jeb, hand me the angel. Steady now. If I fall into this tree, they'll be picking pine needles out of my body for a week. If it happens, just go ahead and bury me, tree and all . . . an awful way to go if you ask me."

A nine-year-old boy, I stepped gingerly on the bottom step, trying not to break the precarious equilibrium which my grandmother had established several feet above. I held the angel up towards her. Half of the angelic yellow hair was gone. The white satin dress was spotted with pine tar, but her porcelain face was beautiful, and my nine-year-old self thought her exquisite.

"Okay, almost got it . . . there, that's it." She let out a sigh of victory and relief. "Now, hold the ladder. I'm coming down."

Once at the bottom, she grabbed me about the shoulders. Her warmth filled me. My head rested against her bony chest.

"I didn't think that your father would be up to putting his all into tree trimming this year." She was chuckling softly, but I could feel her tears running onto my forehead. "That was your mother's angel when she was a little girl, Jeb . . . it sort of reminds me of her."

It was our first Christmas without her. The scene faded. I remembered that the radio in our front parlor had been playing Bing Crosby's "I'll Be Home for Christmas." Even at nine, the song's irony was clear to me.

The remembrance ended. The late Mr. Crosby continued. I was standing in mid-aisle, lost again. Barbie was only a few yards away. One or two minutes and I would be half done with my assigned Christmas buying, but it wasn't to be. As decisively as I had walked into Martin's, I took my hands from the bar of the shopping cart, quietly turned around, located the front door, and left the cart like an abandoned junker. No Barbie. No G.I. Joe. Maybe another night. Maybe Susan would have to do the honors after all.

My key turned in the front door.

"Daddy's home!" I could hear their screams even before my foot crossed the threshold. Susan was arranging a garland in the front hall. She approached with guarded optimism. Her eyebrows raised slightly. Her voice lowered.

"Did you leave it all in the trunk?"

My lips puckered outward. Worse than a recalcitrant fourth-grader, my eyes evaded hers, darting to her work about the house.

"I didn't get anything," I finally stated simply. "I couldn't. I tried. I'll talk to you later about it." Like Susan's, my voice was a whisper, but I strained even with minimal effort. I was in no mood to give or receive a lecture. Susan started to say something, then drew back.

"I understand," she said. I knew that she did.

"Is the snow sticking?" David was the first to reach me. He leaped into my arms, clothed in zip-up footy pajamas, his rubber snow boots flopping half-on and half-off of his feet.

"It's sticking a little." I kissed him. "But not enough for sledding."

"Tomorrow morning?" Annie emerged from the family room. Older than David by four years and a worldly-wise third-grader, Annie was always on the lookout for a snow day. The element of surprise made them almost as good as Christmas itself.

"Don't know," I answered. "Let me get my coat off and warm up a little, and we'll check the weather in a few minutes."

The fire felt good. I held my hands out, then grabbed the poker and stirred the logs. Ashes fell as sparks flew up.

"Stand by to toss a log, Davy," I called out. My boy obliged. He was in the earliest stages of the pyromania all little boys possess in varying degrees.

"Where were you, Daddy?" Annie was baiting me; she knew very well where I was supposed to be. I decided to tell her the truth. "I was at the place where Grandma's buried. I was sort of saying a final goodbye just by myself."

Neither of them knew quite how to respond.

"Tell us a Great-Grandma story." David plopped down next to

me on the couch, and Annie joined us on the other side. David's newly added log had immediately caught fire. Its flame scattered warmth all around us.

"Tell us the story of the flaming Christmas tree," Annie said. "You know, Great-Grandma was just a little girl, and she sat in her bedroom window one cold, cold night . . ." Annie ceased so that I could continue.

"Well," I picked up the plot threads, "Grandma sat admiring the tree in the second-story window just across the street. It was all lit up with beautiful candles, and she could see their glow through the frost that had formed across the window panes . . ."

"And," David added, "it was so cold that Great-Grandma's breath kept covering the window where she sat . . ."

"Yes," I said, "and then, all of a sudden, without any warning . . . the tree shot up in flames before her very eyes."

"And did the neighbor's house burn down?" David asked, even though he knew the answer.

"No," Annie added on cue, leaving no illusion that the story was really mine to tell alone. "The window suddenly flew open. The daddy of the little girl across the street picked up the tree—ornaments and all—and threw it out into the street!" Annie was supremely proud of her story-telling skills.

The three of us stared into the fire, imagining the sight of a flaming Christmas tree.

"More," David insisted. "More stories."

I was sure that I knew more, but I couldn't think of them. Too many reflections during the day had dulled my powers of recall.

"Tell us about the Christmas after Great-Grandma's daddy died," Annie urged. "You know, when Great-Grandma's mommy acted crazy and Great-Grandma's Grandma Bell saved Christmas . . ."

The story existed from my own childhood, told to me nearly thirty years before; it tickled at the back of my mind, but refused to re-emerge.

"I'm not sure I remember, Annie. Did Grandma tell you that story?"

Annie thought for a second. "Yes, she told David and me, right before Thanksgiving."

"How did the story go? Maybe if you start it . . ."

"Well," Annie began, "Great-Grandma's mother loved Great-Grandma's daddy very much. And he drowned in an accident on the river. And that year, Great-Grandma's mother said that Santa had been told not to come and that there wouldn't be any Christmas . . . and Great-Grandma and her little sister cried and cried and cried . . .

until they cried themselves to sleep . . . but when Christmas morning came," Annie stopped, trying to recall a detail that she might have skipped. As she did, like the passage of light from one nearby point to another, the story that I had not heard in almost thirty years came back to me through Annie.

". . . but in the dark of night," I began, "after Grandma and her sister had given up all hope, Grandma's Grandma Bell took Christmas into her own hands. She arrived just before midnight with a doll and a toy piano and a new Sunday dress and shoes . . . more than Grandma and her sister had ever had for Christmas before. But more wonderful than anything else," I paused, shaking my head slowly, "she had remembered the oranges . . . bright and fresh and rare and wonderful . . . more special than sweets or cookies or frankincense, gold, and myrrh . . . brought in by express train from the South . . ."

"And even though Great-Grandma's Grandma Bell had lost a son that year, she remembered the oranges in her granddaughters' stockings." David brought the old story to its close.

The fire was burning well. The evening was young. The roads were passable. There was time. I got up, resettled David and Annie on the couch, and started back toward Susan and the front door.

"I'll be back in an hour or so," I called. Susan nodded knowingly. She had been listening from the hall.

This time my path was clear. As in ancient times, when the wisdom of the elders was passed on to the young through stories, and a little child was said to lead them, so it was that night. When Barbie and G.I. Joe made their appearance on Christmas morning, there would be some oranges in all of our stockings as well . . . so that we might all remember.

CAROLING ON
COMMAND

I was seventeen the year Christmas came of age. It was a time in which my love life was at a low ebb, caught as I was between romances already past and college experiences still a year away. My lackluster love life seemed symbolic of my sense of no longer belonging. I felt a little like Father O'Malley, the priest played by Bing Crosby in those old movies they showed every Christmas. Like the good father, I was a big brother to everyone—the cutest girls in my class included—and to some extent, my priest-like lifestyle played a part in the small drama which shaped that Christmas and all of my Christmases thereafter. Since I was celibate—in those days meaning that I wasn't dating anyone steadily—my only amorous adventures were those of playing Cupid to my good friends.

I will call them Danny and Janet. They married several years later and this thin disguise is for the sake of their children and everyone concerned. I not only introduced Janet to my best friend, Danny, but ever afterward, I somehow became Janet's chauffeur, confidant, and guardian angel.

There was never any hint of attraction between Janet and me (not that Danny would have worried anyway). That one memorable December night I shared with her had nothing to do with teen love. Later, I tried to tell Janet what that wondrous evening had meant to me in a Christmas card which gushed with all of the sentiment I could gather from the pen of a pensive youth, but I guess I didn't get my point across very well. She thought Danny wrote the card.

It all started when Janet's call led me into the embarrassment of Christmas caroling. By some quirk I had neither been caroling before nor seen carolers in my neighborhood. In fact, I thought caroling had ended with Dickens and the nineteenth century. Looking back on it, I had several points in my defense regarding this perception. First, caroling was not generally in vogue. It was an age of growing protest, credibility gaps, and napalm. Second, since my mother's death, my family had never done anything more community-minded than pay their taxes in a timely, if begrudging, manner.

Finally, I attended the Episcopal church, and as I have discovered in the later years of making the rounds—church-wise—Episcopalians are humanitarian, well-bred, and generally too embarrassed to sing. In fact, my own church might well have been called the Church of the Latter Day Faints or the Sect of the Secret Mumblers, since they could not muster a rousing hymn if the second coming hung in the balance.

With this background, there is little wonder that I was gravely shocked when I came to understand that I would have to go caroling if I expected to double that night with Janet, Danny, and Janet's best friend, Susan. Well, actually, Danny was playing a basketball game in a nearby town and would be joining us later. As it would later develop, Susan and I exchanged fewer than twenty-five full sentences in four dates, but at the time, prospects seemed brighter.

"So where are we going after I pick you and Susan up?" I asked Janet over the phone.

"Just pick me up at my house," Janet laughed. "And dress warmly. We're going caroling!" Then she hung up.

It was not an inquiry as to whether I wanted to go caroling; it was a lightly-given command. I hung up the phone, helpless and already embarrassed. An image of myself in a Dickensian cape and long scarf with a tall beaver pelt hat sent a shudder through me. I didn't own such an outfit, but I suddenly imagined some organization so dressing its legions before they sent them out upon the town to make fools of themselves. I pictured myself in a foolish costume, singing off-key carols foolishly, and walking around the streets of my home town like a complete fool. "Fool" was the word most prominently in my thoughts, unless it was "buffoon." What if the police stopped us? After all, Ft. Thomas was a quiet town, with quiet ways, and quiet traditions. It only had a dozen or so registered democrats, and they were quiet about it as well. No, I didn't want to go. I wouldn't go. Of course, I went.

It was a bitterly cold night. The stars seemed to hover just above the tree tops, sparkling in the sky overhead, and fading to a softer glow as they neared the horizon and the city lights of Cincinnati. It was a night for stocking caps and thick sweaters and woolen scarves and union underwear. While it seemed silly enough to even walk from one house to another in such cold, it seemed utterly lunatic to charge around the whole neighborhood, invading one otherwise peaceful home after another singing carols. At least no one would be idiotic enough to wear some flimsy costume on such an arctic night. If they were so inclined, they would be pneumonic after the first verse of the second song. Then perhaps they would forget the whole thing, dismiss it as a quaint, but bad idea, and go straight to someone's party.

With this last hope firmly implanted in my scenario for the evening, I stopped to pick up Janet and Susan. They were dressed warmly, but normally, and I was heartened. Janet directed me to the Christ Evangelical Church, which she attended, and it dawned on me for the first time that this was some type of church activity. I don't know why this hadn't occurred to me earlier, unless it was the result of my sheltered background in the silence of the Episcopalians.

The carolers were gathering in the church basement like commandos in a post-*Guns of Navarone* war movie. Seated at an old upright piano was the father of a friend of mine from school. He wasn't playing, but merely sitting and addressing the gathering of angelic soldiers waiting for their marching orders. As we reached the outer circle of singers, he was passing out the last paperback caroling books. I would have been glad to share, or not sing at all. I looked around and noted the conspicuous absence of my friend whose father was at the center of the group. He had obviously evaded the embarrassment of the evening by some ruse. His father was just finishing his general directives.

"Okay, everybody . . . now, listen up . . ." He had obviously seen action in the military, as evidenced by his inability to get their attention. It was a Friday night, and I was in a church basement—not even my own—listening to a classmate's father sound ineffectual. "Listen, now, you all have booklets . . ." This was obvious. "Hold onto them." He thought we would sell them or burn them for warmth? "Because we need to keep them for next year. Here . . ." he began passing out half-sheets of paper, "is a list of shut-ins who we'll be visiting tonight. At each house we will sing two carols, and two carols only, then move on directly to the next address on the list."

I stood in shock, unable to move. We were going to intrude on the homes of old folks—innocent, tax-paying old folks—whom I did not know, after dark on a Friday night, stand outside their doors, and scare them half to death. Or even all the way to death—I had no adequate gauge of their frailty. I was incredulous. Was this what twentieth-century caroling was all about?

Before I had time to make my excuses and avoid the entire unseemly affair, Janet and Susan had sandwiched me between them, and I was carried in a wave of amateur Mormon Tabernaclers to the parking lot. I had passed the point of no return. Before I knew it, I was driving my father's 1964 Chevy Monza with Janet, Susan, and another couple, careening around the curves of Grand Avenue like a missile bent upon destruction. Two or three cars were in front of me, and another behind, and I felt like a member of a giddy and delirious funeral procession.

"Over there now, yes, that's it . . . right," Janet was shouting in my ear even though she was sitting on the gap between the bucket seats. The car lurched to the right with a life of its own, parked itself, and then disgorged its members in front of a little brick bungalow with a steep front walkway. We all trooped up to the door, and as the assemblage reached their destination, the porch light went on. Our commander turned, and while Janet and Susan and I straggled in from the rear, he brought a pitch pipe to his lips, then stopped before blowing and announced calmly, "Page twenty-one, 'Hark the Herald Angels Sing'." Then he blew on the pipe.

A short, shrill blast pierced the night, and thirty voices, which should have sounded like one, but sounded more like fifty, began to belt out a disjointed version of the well-known carol. I shrunk back to the periphery of this religious mob, hoping that no one would come to the door, and if they did, that they would not call the police. The front door flew open, and a middle-aged couple stood looking out at us, supporting between them a much older lady in a heavy, quilted bathrobe. I was relieved to note that I did not know these people, so I joined the singing in my nasal Episcopalian monotone. The group finished, and the leader, hardly missing a beat, shouted out, "The First Noel," and we were off again.

If one has never heard "The First Noel" sung as a "round," then they have missed a truly spiritual experience. Half the group had not found the carol until "the angels did say," and rather than jump in at that point, they evidenced a solemn belief in their right and duty to sing the carol from the beginning. We bumbled sanctimoniously onward, and I wondered whether I might shrink into the hedge at the foot of the porch without being missed.

Then something very curious happened. The couple did not close their door, or call the police, or even seem to mind that we were disjointed, off-key, and off-pitch (our leader had failed to blow his pipe on top of everything else). The older woman seemed to mind even less. A peaceful smile appeared on her face, then dissolved into a wistful glow, as if she were miles and years away. Then it was over. We were finished. The conclave turned, now with me at the head, and rolled amoeba-like back down to the sidewalk.

"That wasn't so bad," I heard myself saying.

"Well, of course not, silly," Janet laughed. Susan half-smiled and remained, as always, silent. "Did you think it would be painful?" Janet quizzed me.

"Well, I . . . uh . . . didn't know. I thought . . . well, anyway . . . let's go on back to the church and get some punch."

My wise suggestion received not the least attention, and before I could reach my car door, the commander was adroitly spurring us on to new heights.

"Okay, carolers," he chirped, "let's sing while we walk. The next five houses are here on Grand Avenue."

With those words of inspiration, he broke into "God Rest Ye Merry Gentlemen." We were off to new peaks of caroling ecstasy, and I needn't tell you that it didn't stop on Grand Avenue. Three houses on Edwards Court, six on Highland, and four houses on Millers Lane, with a few others sprinkled here and there. It went on for almost two hours, like a Broadway road show, playing one brief stand after another. While the reviews varied, peaking on Millers Lane with a standing ovation from two maiden sisters, the group clearly improved.

We would never be invited to sing at Notre Dame, but delusions of that nature had begun to creep into the collective mind. We had caught that crucial second wind after Edwards Court and were ready to go until midnight.

The bitter cold may have numbed us; I ceased to feel it. Instead of growing tired, we were growing stronger; instead of sounding worse, we were sounding better. As we neared the end of our shut-in checklist, I began feeling very satisfied that I had survived the night with my grand, seventeen-year-old pride intact. I had kept a stiff upper lip, hung to the rear, followed the leader, listened to Janet's street directions, and generally brassed out a bad night. It actually hadn't been so bad.

As we walked up the steps of the first house on the last street, I knew that my abbreviated career as a street performer was almost over. Hot punch and dozens of sugar-sprinkled cookies awaited me. A few houses, maybe a couple of dozen verses of various carols, and another twenty minutes in the twenty-degree weather were all that separated me from the ordeal's end. If I paced myself, I knew I'd make it.

"Okay, we're close to winding up," the general of our little chorale shouted. " 'Hark the Herald' . . . one more time!"

We started with professional verve and punched the old carol through with a certain panache not present at the beginning of our tour. No light went on in the house. No people appeared. No doors opened. I was both confused and a little embarrassed again. Perhaps the shut-ins had shut us out. Or perhaps they were really bogus shut-ins and were at the country club chuckling over Manhattans at the carolers who held the misguided impression that they were enfeebled. We finished "Hark, the Herald" to a darkened porch.

"'O, Little Town of Bethlehem', page thirty-one," the commander called out. There was perplexity written on his face and a quizzical tone in his voice. The group's confidence dipped as they fumbled through their books and began singing. At least the previously man- dated "two carol rule" would save us from any further discomfort.

Then, just as we were zipping into the final "the hopes and fears of all the years . . ." the porch light came on and the front door creaked slowly open. In the diffused light thrown from the dirty glass shade, an ancient couple stood smiling at us behind their storm door, their hands cupped to their ears, the old woman bundled in a heavy, knitted shawl, the old man lost within the folds of a thick wool cardigan. Around the white collar of her blouse was tied a red satin ribbon, and attached to his plaid flannel shirt was a clip-on bow tie, tied so as to look like two sprigs of holly. They had been waiting for us. They simply hadn't heard us.

Their breath formed an ever-increasing sea of frost on the inside of their storm door as they stood and watched us. They were waiting for us to begin, just as our stunning rendition of "O Little Town" ended. Our stalwart field marshal presented a goofy grin.

"Well, Mr. Bundt . . . Mrs. Bundt . . . Merry Christmas. See you next year."

With that he turned, and with him, the rest of the loyal troupe. All, that is, except for one lowly private in the great army of angelic heralders . . . one insignificant deserter who realized in the flash of a millisecond that perhaps Mr. and Mrs. Bundt might not be there the next Christmas. In the flash of the next millisecond, he realized that for a brief moment in the history of mankind, the cup of human kindness had been entrusted to his care. He drank of it, and throwing caution to the wind, determined to pass it on. He stood his ground, turned traitor to the iron-clad two carol rule, and opened his mouth. Words came forth.

"Good King Wenceslas looked out," I began, "on the Feast of Ste- phen. And the snow lay round about . . ." The group halted in its push for the sidewalk, then turned and stared in wonder. They were shocked. The two carol rule had been broken. And by a stranger. But before I could belt out ". . . crisp and fresh and even," Janet and

Susan had joined me, then a half a dozen others, and finally the group leader himself. His look of horror at my boldness faded on the words, "Brightly shone the moon that night, though the frost was cruel . . ."

Mr. Bundt and Mrs. Bundt held tightly to each other and stared out at us from their foggy vantage point. As the words "When a poor man came in sight, gathering winter fuel" were sung, I thought for a moment they were looking at me.

The group leader glanced my way and smiled, still, like myself, unsure about the facts surrounding my defection from protocol, but not unhappy with the result. "The First Noel?" he inquired of me.

"Number fifteen," I grinned in reply, and now the entire host of cherubims and seraphims held forth with, "The First Noel, the angels did say . . ." Janet moved over next to me and gently squeezed my hand.

I remember very little about the rest of the evening. No one rebuked me for my abuse of the "two carol" rule. In fact, they said nothing. A few gentle pats on the back told me all I needed to know. Janet met Danny later, and they blissfully departed. I took Susan home, and, true to form, did not dare kiss her good night. I went on to college the next year, and for all of the following years of school, I would be too displaced from the mainstream of small-town life to go caroling with the valiant singers of Christ Evangelical. I never saw Mr. and Mrs. Bundt again.

But I remember them. Every time I end up carrying my little boy through the last half of church caroling in our neighborhood. Every time I troop clumsily into a nursing home or some overheated little house to fill it with off-key singing. Every time I hear "Good King Wenceslas." And I think of the dumb luck and brazen nerve that catapulted an insecure seventeen-year-old onto a slightly higher plane of being that special Christmas.

SHORT'S STORY

The red rear lights of the car ahead flashed like a Christmas tree, and Jack Short jammed on the brakes of his beat-up, yellow Volkswagen bug. "Why me?" he muttered. "Why did the Old Man send me to cover a Christmas story about that crumby little church?" he thought. The Volkswagen slid on a thin layer of ice and stopped six inches from the bumper of the bulky Chevrolet in front. "Okay," Short grumbled to himself. "Mind on the road. Get back to the office, then worry about the crumby story."

Short scratched his wiry black beard, ran his right hand over a gradually thinning shock of hair, and settled his six-foot, five-inch frame over the wheel of the Volkswagen. For a moment, his thoughts raced ahead to the poker game already in progress. His buddies were undoubtedly well into the first fifth of Jack Daniels, and Short had missed both the first hand and the first fifth. What was Christmas for, at least this year, if you couldn't get time off to have a drink or two and a game of cards with the guys? Especially since his grim, silent smirk could always hide the knowledge of a good hand.

But the Old Man had said, "Short, I need a story for the home edition. Christmas seems to be coming a little hard to you this year—what with the divorce and all. You'll be up late Christmas Eve anyway with your friends on the sports page, so do me a favor first and cover the service at 45th and Vincent. It's right in the middle of the projects.

It's a little place called the Church of the Holy Gospel. I don't know if you'll find anything, but I need a good human interest piece. So try real hard to find *something*."

Short had found the building, anyway. Ancient, red brick turning to dust. Just big enough for its small, aging, black congregation, a smattering of their grandchildren, one octogenarian minister, and Short. Short had taken one look around as he walked in and knew it was on its last legs. And he was supposed to weave a Christmas story out of that collection of brick and human rubble.

The Volkswagen sputtered to a rough idle as Short stopped at the rail crossing. He lit a cigarette and leaned his long torso backwards as the slow freight clicked its monotonous rhythm. Jack Short glanced at his watch. Another ten minutes would be lost from deadline while the endless line of boxcars crept through the city on its way north.

Short looked down at his notes, opened on the passenger's seat next to him. "Reverend Lyman Brown, Jr . . . black nativity . . . 'O Holy Night' (hymn) . . ." There was more. But it didn't constitute the pieces of a recognizable puzzle. For a good number of the congregation it was probably their last Christmas. Cold, disease, and hunger would take some of them before spring. It was most certainly the last Christmas for the church. The pews were cracked, half painted, askew. The plaster on the back wall was almost entirely gone. The oaken beams overhead creaked with the passing wind or a gospel sung loudly.

The lonely freight train paraded on past Jack. He took his pencil from the ring in his notebook and began scribbling. "Not a bad little service." He crossed it out. "The Church of the Holy Gospel at 45th and Vincent paid a happy birthday last night to Baby Jesus. Time has just about said good-bye to the little church." The sentences were awkward, but he liked the lead.

Jack was not immune to good-byes this year. His father had died the previous May. Diane had left in October. It would all be final by New Year's. He knew all about good-byes and endings. But Christmas stories. It was the one thing he didn't need. The one thing most distant from his own sadness. Christmas stories. And the Old Man hadn't sent him for a normal, simple Christmas story about canned goods for shut-ins or snowmen on a white Christmas or the sick child that gets a puppy. No, the Old Man had sent him specifically to that crumby little hopeless church.

"I don't know what kind of *something*," the Old Man had said in response to Short's exasperated question. "You go and tell me. You're the bright Harvard graduate. I'm the editor, and you're the reporter, and I'm sending you. That's the way it works. So move it.

The sooner you leave, the sooner you'll be back. Besides, you're covering an 11 P.M. service and it's almost ten now. Have a good time." The wiry, graying editor had coughed in brief, and final, punctuation and returned to his work.

At 11:05 P.M., Jack Short had found himself uncomfortably Caucasian, bearded, underdressed (poor as the men around him were, they wore old, dark suits and white starched shirts), and a head above the rest of the congregation at the Church of the Holy Gospel. Nonetheless, he sat, stood, kneeled, and even sang, after a fashion, at the right times. Annie Henderson, 84, sat to his right. She smiled at him and smacked her gums throughout the service. George Friend, 72, sat to his left. He simply nodded solemnly as Jack sat down, then glanced over occasionally between the choruses of "Go Tell It on The Mountain" and nodded again.

Perched between Annie and George, Jack had pressed his lips together tightly to suppress a smile during the nativity play that filled the middle of the service. If the whole situation weren't so pathetic, he had thought, it really would be a delight. The children, ranging in age from four to twelve, were all in the play. They punched it through with more energy than talent, announcing their lines with great solemnity. The language had obviously been drawn from the King James Version of the New Testament, and bore no resemblance to the local street vernacular. "Thou art Mary, the mother of our Lord and Savior, Jesus Christ." The left corner of Short's mouth inched upward. He pulled it back down.

Reverend Brown gave a sermon on the congregation's need to be generous with the needy; the irony of the plea was apparently lost on everyone but Short. An overweight woman in her seventies played "Away in the Manger" on the piano and sang, while the children brought ornaments for a dry, spindly pine tree half resting on the choir rail. When the carol was over the congregation rose, hugged each other, gave Jack a few friendly pats, sang "Hark the Herald Angels" together, and filed away into the dark, empty spaces where houses had once stood around the church.

The gate at the crossing sprang upwards and the clanging ceased. Short ended his reminiscence and restarted his car, shifting it into second gear as he crossed the tracks. The shudder he had experienced watching the last of the older people disappear into the early Christmas morning passed through him again. A dying church, a dying congregation, an urban "renewed" neighborhood . . . yet a service pouring from the collective heart of those with whom he had shared Christmas Eve. Jack tried to get his emotions back under control, but failed.

Too many deaths—of people, of relationships—had filled his own life recently.

A shock of anger at the Old Man followed the shudder he had felt a moment earlier. The paper had a staff of writers who could have done the story without problems, complications, or personal life crises. They would have verbally painted the old, decaying church in crisp, concise terms and found something colorful about the service. Enough, in any event, for the morning edition.

Short turned left and began the boulevard's ten-block stretch towards the office. He still didn't have a story. A well-dressed couple stepped out without warning from the curb. Short down-shifted, and the brakes squealed. The man in a black tuxedo and tie and the woman in furs proceeded without a glance at Short. Jack grinned briefly. It was the publisher and his wife. If he'd hit them it would have at least been news. But it didn't help his church story any.

Short parked his car, emerged from under its canvas top, checked in with security, and pushed the elevator button for the fourth floor. The door slid open, revealing the city room only half lit, silent but for the hum of the wire service machines, a low murmur of voices in the far west cubicles, and the constant drone of the main computer terminal. Jack Short was overwhelmed by the depression which had haunted him on the trip back from the service.

In the corner of the semi-dark room, one bright desk lamp burned on the Old Man's desk. The Old Man stood with his back to Short, hands thrust in his pockets, staring out into the city. Jack started slowly towards the office, his gym shoes squeaking against the tile floor of the city room.

Short cleared his throat. The Old Man didn't budge. Jack moved closer, and the Old Man reached into his shirt pocket for a cigarette.

"Well, how's tricks in the high rent district?" the Old Man grunted, pivoting on his right foot as Jack Short stepped inside the cluttered office.

"Depressing," Jack offered. "What were you expecting?"

"I'm expecting a story for the home edition. What have you got?" The Old Man removed a Zippo lighter from his hip pocket and lit his Pall Mall.

"Damn little." Jack bristled.

"Well, tell me what you have got. I've got to call downstairs in a minute."

"A run-down little church. A bunch of old people. A smattering of little kids. A nativity play. Some Christmas carols. A piano out of tune."

"And what else?" the Old Man interrupted.

"And what else was I supposed to find? What the hell do you think I was supposed to find?" Jack paused, his face flushed. "Should I write a story about dreams that were? Hopes and lives and a neighborhood that's dying? A church that's going to join the debris around it by spring? That'll make a great Christmas story!" The assignment was no longer a minor irritation. Too many dead people and dead relationships in his own life had interposed themselves between Jack Short and his usually good-humored sense of the absurd. He threw his notebook on the table.

The city editor picked it up, thumbed through it quickly, and looked up at Short rising almost a foot above him. "What about the nativity play? I mean the Victorian language of it. What about the Christmas tree and the old woman playing "Away in the Manger" while the little kids put the ornaments on it? Isn't there a story there?"

"You summed it up," Jack said. "That's it. That's all there was. No more. Nothing special. Nothing much to catch your eye. Just a crumby little dying . . ." Jack stopped.

"Hold on a second. I didn't tell you about the language in the play, or the kids hanging the ornaments. And I didn't write it in my notes. If you already had all of that stuff, why did you send me down there?"

"I didn't have it."

"What do you mean you didn't . . ." Jack began, then stopped, catching a gleam in the Old Man's eye. There was a moment of silence. Only the computer terminal kept purring away.

"I didn't have it," the Old Man repeated. "At least I never knew for sure. And I never wrote the story. You have it. Or at least you have a lot of it. Maybe not quite enough yet." The Old Man paused, inhaled on his cigarette, and began again. "I had a lot of it. But that was thirty years ago. Right after Mary and the kids went back to live in Chicago. And my editor sent me to the Church of the Holy Gospel when I wanted nothing more than to go on an all-nighter with two guys from the city desk. Well, I dutifully recorded the dying little church, the decaying bricks and timbers, the ancient congregation, the little kids doing that stilted, outdated nativity and then decorating the tree. And I walked in here just like you did tonight.

"Of course, my editor was smarter than you and I. He knew Lyman Brown. He had done his research way ahead of time. And he knew first-hand the strength of that drafty, broken-down church.

"He told me then. He said, 'Bub, that church has been there for a hundred years. It's been on its last leg for fifty, and it will still be there when I'm dead and you're old.'

"Well, Jack, I took him at his word. But I never wrote the story. Like a good reporter, you've gotta ask the right questions, follow your leads, double check your sources, and believe what you're writing. I didn't have a double check and I wouldn't have believed—maybe known, but not believed—what I *could* have written. Then I saw you dragging around here this last week, and I remembered the story I never wrote. And I had to have my double check, Jack. I had to have the proof of time . . . if it was all there to be proven." The Old Man paused. "Now all the facts are in."

Jack slipped slowly into the editor's desk chair. His anger, frustration, and even the slight, unspoken fear he had always had of the Old Man dissolved. In the empty space which these departed feelings left, a new emotion began to overwhelm Jack, sweeping through him like air rushing inward to fill a void. A bond of love and friendship between the older man and the younger was forged and solidified in that moment, and Jack sensed that it would last for the rest of their lives.

The Old Man cleared his throat. "Now, Short, we've both got more facts than we had before. And the home edition needs a good human interest story. And I'm the editor, and you're not. So write me a story, Short. One that you believe in. And if it's a story about death and decay—fine, go ahead and write it. But you've got all of the necessary facts now. And you've got an hour to get it downstairs." He stubbed his cigarette out abruptly, then turned away from Jack and looked out of the window again. "Then maybe, if you'd like, we'll grab a bite of breakfast somewhere."

Jack remembered the poker game that would still be in its early stages. And he remembered the breakfasts his father used to make for him. "Yeah," Jack said. "I'll see you downstairs in an hour."

The poker game on the east side of town was winding to a close when Jack woke up, tasted the maple syrup still sticking to his mustache, and groggily got the morning paper from the back door of his apartment. "The Church of the Holy Gospel at 45th and Vincent paid a happy birthday last night to Baby Jesus. And as He has done for one hundred and thirty years, and probably will do for one hundred and thirty more, Jesus paid back his respects to his little church of hope and joy. . . ." Jack Short smiled a broad, bright grin. "If only I'd had another hour to work on that introduction," he thought.

THE LAST
APPOINTMENT
BEFORE CHRISTMAS

T he closing credits rolled down the twelve-inch television screen. The old crooner appeared in front of a Las Vegas casino, wearing a Santa Claus cap and tuxedo. "God bless you all," he mumbled, running the words together, then with a nod to the band leader began to sing "Have Yourself a Merry Little Christmas." Vince Hoffman slammed his finger down on the "Stop" button of the VCR, rubbed his eyes, opened them slowly, and murmured, "What a piece of crap." Vince stared around the fourth floor newsroom of the *Times-Clarion*. It was 8:00 A.M. on the day before Christmas Eve. While none of the staff reporters were supposed to have taken time off, he had nevertheless watched the fourth floor take on the serenity of a funeral parlor as gradually from Monday through Wednesday desks became miraculously clear and tidy. Vince chuckled. The real news media were covering actual "Christmas stories," while he was stuck reviewing "Christmas in Las Vegas."

Vince stretched his six-foot, four-inch frame, shuffled to the coffee machine, and exchanged a belated "good morning" with the receptionist.

"Should I watch the Las Vegas Christmas special tonight, Vince?" she asked.

Vince's face broke into a slow smile. "Not if you value your sense of Christmas."

"Ohhhh . . ." she said. "Does this one, by any chance, lean back on its hind legs and bark?"

"You've said it all," Vince laughed. "Now I must go fill sixty-five lines to reach the same conclusion." He paused and ran his hand through his thick brown hair. "Seriously, have a Merry Christmas."

"You too, Vince."

Vince went back to his desk, flicked on the word processor, and began typing two-finger style. "While admittedly more authentic to the desert setting of Bethlehem, Las Vegas is no holy land . . ." He paused to think, looking down at his desk calendar. The appointment for 2:00 P.M. was marked in red: "Mark Dudley's office." Vince glanced back at the screen, shook his head, and continued.

＊＊＊＊＊＊＊

It was 8:35 A.M. in the accounting offices of Walker-Ross when Frank Counts put down his pencil, put out his cigarette, and stood up for the first break of the morning. "Why is Mr. Tobin leaving for Bermuda this afternoon?" Counts thought. "And doesn't he have enough money to buy his wife a new diamond necklace with or without our opinion on the deductibility of his trip as a business expense?" Frank had been at the office since 6:30 A.M. By 9:30 A.M., he had to notify the client. To deduct or not to deduct. By 10:45 A.M., he would be meeting with his senior partner on last week's audit results of Beckley Distillers. Noon was set aside for shopping. The last appointment was at 2:00 P.M.

It was about time for Frank to think about Christmas. Nancy had done most of the shopping for the children already. That was his biggest regret about the rush this year. The three weeks before Christmas had passed in the basement of the Beckley Distillery Company, surrounded by Christmas cases of bourbon earmarked as special gifts. Frank laughed at the recollection. None of the cases bore *his* name. Surrounded by all of the "Christmas spirits," he couldn't drink the bourbon, let alone feel the "spirit." Thank goodness that imprisonment had ended. By the end of the audit, only five days were left before Christmas. Nancy had filled in for him through all those weeks, and her gift should be special this year. "Well," Frank thought, "that's two other deadlines away."

Frank stared out the window of the thirty-fifth floor, then started down the long hall toward his third cup of coffee. He checked his watch. It was 8:40. A volley of laughter emitted from the kitchen and poured into the silent and otherwise staid halls of Walker-Ross.

Frank straightened his body to its full five feet, eight inches and, assuming a talented impression of Ebenezer Scrooge, stormed into the kitchen. "All right. What right or reason have you to laugh? Are there no prisons? The Treadmill and the Poor Law, are they still in operation?" Their laughter mounted as Frank got into the role. "Bah, humbug!" he snorted.

Still snickering, they pulled him over. "Do you remember last year's Christmas party, Frank?" A group guffaw erupted. "Remember Rhonda the Red-Nosed Reindeer?"

Another broke in, his voice lowering, "She was so far gone she passed out in the main conference room."

"But not before she spilled eggnog down the front of her blouse and took it off and hung it in the planters," whispered a third.

"Yeah," Frank remarked, "Santa took off his beard, and we covered her up with it until one of the girls got her dressed again."

Though he laughed along with them, Frank started running over in his mind the excuse he would have for not returning to the annual office party after his two o'clock appointment. One more year of Rhonda the Red-Nosed Reindeer and he would give up Christmas forever. They all meant well, Frank thought. They just seemed to have missed the point.

✳ ✳ ✳ ✳ ✳ ✳ ✳

Mark Dudley hit the first light on Main Street just as it turned amber. He weaved to the right around a slow-moving motorcycle and looked ahead. "Only two more shopping days," the disc jockey chided. Mark's finger punched another button as he impulsively sought delivery from further gloomy reminders of a season that had passed too soon. An attorney-at-law, he sought an extension that no one could grant. He last thought of Christmas shopping just before the Smithfield products liability case went to trial. That was two weeks ago. Mark had barely realized Thanksgiving was over and now Christmas was rushing at him by surprise.

Mark shifted down to third gear. With the fear of being unprepared for Christmas, his speed had crept beyond 45 mph. The next light turned green while he was halfway through the intersection. "Lucky," Mark thought. "No cross traffic. And no cops with nothing better to do than watch for fools on their way to work."

Maybe he could find something for his mother that evening. Katherine's gift was waiting to be picked up on the way home. Thank God Bailey's Department Store stayed open until seven.

Had Katherine already purchased a gift for his sister? It wasn't Mark's first Christmas by proxy, but he hoped it would be his last.

Of course, he had had the same hope three years running. "Why do the courts schedule so many trials in December?" he wondered. He knew the answer without thinking twice. Juries find for plaintiffs at Christmas time; judges like to see cases get settled out of court; so my defense clients settle more often, for more money. It was a calculated business expense during December.

Mark weaved in and out of the last block of traffic and turned right. On the radio he heard the version of "Jingle Bells" performed by barking dogs. He remembered first hearing it years before on the way home from school. "Now, that's the spirit," Mark thought. He began to concentrate on the bright side of the next three days. Barring disaster, he and Katherine would have a quiet Christmas Eve together, then attend midnight mass at the cathedral. He had fought for the concession, knowing that they would have to drive eight hours on Christmas day to Katherine's parents'. An eight hour drive wasn't so bad. Mark remembered driving home in the snow from college on Christmas. It was the same trip where he'd heard the barking dogs. It had taken twenty hours, and a tractor trailer had almost taken his life. No, eight hours wasn't bad. It could be a lot worse.

He pulled his car into the parking garage, parked, and reached for his briefcase in the back seat. All of the materials for his two o'clock appointment were collected and ready for presentation. Mark glanced at his watch. It was 8:45 A.M., and he knew of at least three phone calls from the previous day that should be returned before his 9:30 deposition.

The elevator bell rang in less than thirty seconds. Mark got in and it shot to the twelfth floor. "Everyone's clearing out early," Mark thought to himself as he passed through the front door into the reception area, said hello, picked up his messages, and stopped for a mug of coffee before he reached his office. He blew away the steam from the rim of the mug while he thumbed through the pink phone slips that had been recorded that morning. Two calls could wait. One was urgent. Now he had four phone calls to make before 9:30.

The fluorescent overhead lights flickered drearily to life as he touched the switch. Mark winced. "Not this morning," he muttered, turning on his table lamp and flipping off the overhead lights. Mark reached for the phone and punched in the first call of the day. "It's show time," he whispered to himself.

∗ ∗ ∗ ∗ ∗ ∗ ∗

The morning of December 23 passed uneventfully but with anticipation. At the new Center City Mall the construction crew took its first break, and in groups of three and four figured the amount of their last take-home pay of the year and where it would be spent.

Cindy Grimes brushed away freshly-cut hair from the lapels of her first appointment and glanced at a schedule book filled with her white-collar clientele until 4:00 P.M. After four, the day was strictly her own to decide which of ten office party invitations she would honor. Being an attractive downtown barber had its advantages.

The tellers at the First Citizens Bank were even friendlier than usual and wanted even more to give out extra cash to their poorer clientele. They wouldn't, of course, but they wanted to.

At City Hall, a skeleton staff answered phone calls. The Mayor was in Colorado skiing with his family, ostensibly attending a conference on urban development. The taxpayers would not complain.

Schuler, the jeweler, was trying to engrave in one day more gold-filled belt buckles than he would see in any given month—other than December—and Fred Clauss, the baker, was running a special on Christmas cookies. It was, on the whole, a normal late-December business day.

****

By lunchtime downtown was ready for a break. Vince Hoffman took a bite out of a pastrami sandwich at Toots' Deli and washed it down with a mammoth swig of Coca-Cola. He glanced up from the deli bar at the round, grease-covered clock over the cash register. "That clock must have twenty years of build-up on it," he thought. It was 12:15, and by 12:45 he would need to rewrite the story about the Las Vegas Christmas special. "I don't care if you didn't like the show. That review wasn't just stinging, it was vicious," the editor had barked. "Clean it up and no jokes about the Las Vegas mafia." Vince would have to hurry to be at Dudley's law offices by 2:00. He crammed one last chunk of pastrami into his mouth, put his money on the counter, wished Louise, the counter cook, a Merry Christmas and headed for the door.

****

Frank Counts carefully removed the second of two oat and honey granola bars from the vendor pack he had picked up from the machine on the third floor. Less care would mean more crumbs to clean up. "Thank God they invented Diet Coke to replace Tab," he thought as he sipped between calculations. The carbonated, caffeinated, caramel-colored water had the wonderful effect of deceiving Frank into believing that he was staying trim, settling his stomach, and staying awake in one wholesome sip. Normally Frank had no such delusions, but this December 23 he could use a little self-deception to get him through to his two o'clock appointment. It was at least the downward slide. By 12:30 he would be finished with the revisions on the Beckley Distillery audit and out in the fresh air to buy Nancy's Christmas gift.

Frank was half an hour late escaping from the office, but at least he knew where he was going. Four blocks through a brisk wind, past the newly constructed shopping mall (new hope for downtown, the Chamber insisted), immediately beyond Bailey's Department Store and a sharp left into Schuler's Jewelry. He went directly to the estate and antique jewelry in the rear of the store. He gazed down at a cream-colored, cameo brooch and tried to stop calculating that proportion of Mr. Tobin's trip to Bermuda which was deductible. Two months before he had seen the brooch and failed to buy it early. All the way to Schuler's he had had the nagging fear that he would be too late.

"I'll take the brooch. The cameo, that is."

"A nice piece, young man," said one of Schuler's younger assistants, who was probably no more than sixty-five. Ironically, Schuler was supervising the engraving of a belt buckle that Nancy would give Frank after the children were in bed on Christmas Eve.

"Thank you. Can you gift wrap it, please?"

"Surely," said the old man. Frank watched nervously as the clerk walked to the back of the room and, thank heavens, presented the brooch to Schuler's daughter for wrapping. Frank remembered that the same old fellow had wrapped a ring the year before. It had looked like the work of a well-intentioned five-year-old.

Relieved, relaxed and ready to retrace his route down Fourth Avenue, Frank wrote out his check, placed the package, which was more bow than box, in his overcoat and left. The corner clock outside Bailey's Department Store struck once. It was 1:30. Frank picked up his pace, walked when the signs said "DON'T WALK," and avoided anything but a side glance at the window displays on the way back to the office. He still had a two o'clock appointment.

＊＊＊＊＊＊＊＊

Mark Dudley nervously fingered his napkin while Ralph Mann methodically dug into a generous serving of amaretto and ice cream. Mann was a pleasant enough fellow, regional claims supervisor for the Physician's Mutual Insurance Company (an increasingly frequent client), and he had an excellent sense of when to settle and when to try a case. But where was his sense of moderation? Well, Mark thought, Ralph deserved a perk or two like anyone else. Of course, this was his fourth course, his third scotch and water, and worse, he was ending the second hour of lunch.

Mark glanced at his watch. It was 1:35. Mann caught him from the corner of his eye.

"Got something coming up, Mark?" he asked.

"Oh," Mark began, "a two o'clock appointment . . . back at the office."

"No problem." Mann smiled and licked his spoon clean after the last bite. "You're a good host and a good lawyer, Mark," Mann said, lifting his glass. "Merry Christmas and let's get going." As the ice tinkled against the side of the tumbler, Ralph Mann finally finished his scotch and, with it, lunch. Mark Dudley was on his way to his long-standing appointment at 2:00 P.M.

✳ ✳ ✳ ✳ ✳ ✳ ✳ ✳

When the clock at Trinity Church finally struck two, Mark Dudley was midstride through the large mahogany double doors of his law office. Vince Hoffman had miraculously beaten him there, raising his eyes from a magazine as he came in.

The receptionist looked up scornfully. "Mr. Hoffman has been here for five minutes." Her voice and demeanor implied five years. Mark ignored her.

The door opened again, barely missing Mark Dudley where he stood.

"I'm sorry, Mark," Frank Counts apologized, then turned and looked across the reception area. "Good to see you again, Vince." Frank moved over to shake hands with Vince Hoffman as Mark removed his coat and asked the others for theirs.

They made an interesting trio: Vince Hoffman—shaggy hair and mustache, tall and a little stoop-shouldered; Frank Counts—clean-shaven and trim, very tailored, a full eight inches shorter than Vince; and Mark Dudley—a six-foot compromise between the two, horn-rimmed glasses and a receding hair line that he accentuated with a cut reminiscent of Gary Cooper.

"The east conference room is ready," Mark explained as he led them down the long corridor of volume after volume of reported cases. "Just one quick stop here . . ." he ducked into his office and picked up his briefcase, "and we're ready."

"Lisa," Mark turned to his secretary, "I'll be in conference for the next two hours. No calls. Absolutely. I'll be in the office past 6:00, and we'll be through before 5:30, so if it's urgent I'll call them back."

"Yes, Mr. Dudley." Lisa smiled. She knew by Mark's voice that he was serious.

Mark Dudley turned the large brass door handle downward, swung the heavy door open, and guided his conferees to the large oval table which nearly filled the room. Mark closed the door behind him and placed his briefcase on the edge of the conference table. He adjusted the combination slightly, flipped the latches at both ends, and opened the top.

He paused for a moment and looked around. The world outside slipped silently away, and a room which had seldom housed anything friendlier than a meeting of the partnership was suddenly overcome by a pronounced quiet. Phones ceased ringing, senior partners lost access, and editors fell out of sight, as if one large collective heart had slowed in pace to a soft, steady murmur.

"My dear friends," Mark began. "This Christmas we shall begin with a glass of my favorite port," and Mark Dudley withdrew three short-stemmed glasses and a bottle of fine ruby port. He poured each a glass and passed them quietly around.

"A toast," he said. "To a Christmas tradition well saved," he paused, "and well served."

Vince Hoffman raised his glass. "To our twenty-second anniversary, if anyone's counting."

Frank Counts looked aside to see if this was aimed at him. He laughed. "From the loneliest freshman at Wesleyan College to the loneliest freshmen at Dartmouth and Duke. To the Christmas of 1968 when student strikes were brewing and my girlfriend broke up with me and shattered my heart."

"To our first December 23 . . . up in your attic, Mark."

"And to Jimmy Stewart and Donna Reed . . . without whom we might have spent the night talking about *all* the girls who never appreciated us," added Vince.

"Speaking of *It's A Wonderful Life*," Mark grinned, "by the wonders of VHS, VCR, hocus-pocus, and the little clerk who forgot to renew the copyright, we will fill our time together, in part, with those same old characters." Like a self-satisfied magician, Mark Dudley drew a video cartridge from his briefcase, walked to the cabinet that was set into the book shelves which covered one wall, and pushed aside a panel to reveal a television and video machine. He popped in the cartridge and turned to his friends.

"I've got to admit this conference room is not up to par with my dusty old attic. But it will have to do. Anyway, I am too old-fashioned just to show Christmas on TV. So let's read first." As his two friends nodded assent, Mark Dudley went back to his briefcase, took out a book, sat down, and began to read excerpts.

"Marley was dead, to begin with. There is no doubt about that . . ." Mark began, his voice a steady, soothing baritone. Vince Hoffman and Frank Counts leaned back in their chairs, relaxing into an afternoon nestled between timenotes and deadlines. Mark skipped from one stave of *A Christmas Carol* to the next.

" 'Who are you?' 'Ask me who I *was*.' 'Who *were* you then?' said Scrooge, raising his voice. '. . . in life I was your partner, Jacob Marley.' " Mark thumbed onward, shifting to the scene where little Fan, Scrooge's sister, came to bring him home for Christmas and then to the scene when Fan died in childbirth. Mark's voice broke slightly. He cleared his throat to cover it, sipped his port, and moved on to the final scenes and the whole of stave five, ending with:

"Scrooge was better than his word. He did it all, and infinitely more; and to Tiny Tim, who did NOT die, he was a second father. He became as good a friend, as good a master, and as good a man as the good old city knew, or any other good old city, town or borough in the good old world . . ."

Mark paused and cleared his throat again.

Vince raised his glass. "You're awful sappy for an attorney." His own voice broke just slightly.

"More port," Frank chuckled. "Or we'll never make it through *It's A Wonderful Life* without a box of Kleenex."

Mark Dudley laughed, wiping a tear from the corner of his eye, then finished. ". . . and it was always said of him that he knew how to keep Christmas well, if any man alive possessed the knowledge. May that be truly said of us, and all of us! And so, as Tiny Tim observed, God Bless Us every one!"

"Well done," Vince critiqued.

"On to Jimmy and Donna," Frank urged.

"Another round first," said Mark, filling their glasses with port and moving back to the cabinet where he turned on the television and pressed the "Start" button on the VCR. He lifted his glass. "Here's to progress . . . and the past."

✳ ✳ ✳ ✳ ✳ ✳ ✳

On the thirty-fifth floor of the First Citizen's Bank Building, Frank Counts' supervising partner read with satisfaction the results of the Beckley audit. On the fourth floor of the *Times-Clarion*, Vince

Hoffman's editor read with relief the revised review of "Christmas in Las Vegas." Outside of a law firm's closed conference room doors, phone messages continued to amass for Mark Dudley. And within the conference room—as they had in the attic of Mark Dudley's house on Maple Street—three old high school friends dismissed the world around them and shared their annual appointment on the twenty-third day of December.

THE WISDOM
OF THE MAGI

Since childhood I had dreamed of a white Christmas. Every song relied on it. Every fantasy incorporated its calming beauty. Every miracle, every angel's visitation, and every transformation of the soul was barely possible without a blanket of two or more inches of pure white magic. Now the reality of that dream was threatening Christmas for my entire family as I watched the snow falling steadily outside my office window.

We are, as a good friend puts it, a blended family. While I have always thought the term more appropriate to Scotch whiskey, it means that Liza is my daughter by a prior marriage. Joey is the son of my wife, Beth. Liza lives with her mother in Cincinnati. Ordinarily the hundred miles from Louisville to Cincinnati is traveled with ease. At worst it is a tedious trip. That is, when the weather is good. On the rare occasion when snow or sleet descends, the journey can become as dangerous as a voyage to the North Pole.

The city below me was evolving from gray to white. With that evolution, it became more and more likely that Joey and I would miss Liza's first-grade Christmas pageant. It was 9:30 in the morning, and four hours seemed barely enough time to make the trip if the storm continued.

"Did you hear? Operation Snowfall is in effect!" At the prospect of leaving work just moments after arriving, my secretary was blatantly euphoric. Her voice reverberated through the halls and startled me back to the confines of my office. She stood in my doorway with a well-I-can't-help-it-but-I-guess-we-all-have-to-go-home smile on her face. I couldn't blame her. On any other day I would have felt the same way.

"Are you sure?" I asked guardedly.

"You bet!" Her brightly rouged cheeks alternately soared and sagged, depending on whether she was illustrating her sincere desire to go home or her guilt-born loyalty to the office. "I heard it on the radio just now."

"What else did they say?"

"Six inches by noon. More snow tonight . . ." her voice was rising with Wagnerian splendor, "Stay off the streets. Go home and get warm. Hoorah!"

I looked at her, one eyebrow slightly arched, my lips held firmly together. Her eyes darted to the side. She looked slightly embarrassed.

"Since when are you such a Scrooge?" Knowing me fairly well, however, she quickly regained the spirit of the occasion. "I thought you liked the snow!"

"I love snow . . . when I don't have to drive in, through, and over it."

"Well, why don't you just postpone your appointment?"

"It's not an appointment, exactly . . . it's my little girl's Christmas pageant. Besides, she's coming home with me for the weekend. It'll be our last before Christmas."

"Oh . . . I forgot . . ." Her joy expelled like steam from a teakettle. She knew that Liza lived in Cincinnati. Divorced herself, she knew the melodramas it could create. "Maybe if you called her . . . to explain you'll come tomorrow."

"I can't, really. She's at school."

Her face lost its light and her shoulders slumped forward.

"Then I suppose you're going?"

"I don't have any choice." In the very moment I said it, I knew that I was lying. I had a choice, and it was by far the wiser course: stay off the roads.

"Well, the wise men had a pretty rough trip at Christmas time . . . and they made it. . . ." Her voice trailed off as she realized that I could see no useful analogy between the plight of the Magi and myself. She could hardly begin to sense how unwise I was feeling.

"Right. Well, at least I won't need a star to find the way."

"Yeah . . . well, I'd better get the last few letters in the mail." We were both at a loss for anything meaningful to say. "Whatever you decide to do, Liza will understand. She's an awfully bright little girl."

"Thanks. I mean it," I said. She turned from the doorway and disappeared.

I turned back to the window, watching, pondering whether I even had a choice. The slush twenty stories below must surely be ice twenty miles to the north. If I waited until late afternoon the roads would probably be clear. Common sense and adult reason told me not to go that morning. Liza's pleading voice on the telephone the night before and Joey's insistent yearning compelled a different course. And there was more. Darker and more selfish, there was my own desire not to be undone by nature, my own resentment at the prospect of not delivering the expected, my own stubborn determination not to allow divorce to hamper our family's love. There was simply more at stake than would justify a wise man's caution. Liza had referred to her younger brother as a "half" only once. I had smiled and noted that Joey was a whole person, just as she was to him. A full-fledged brother could and should come to her school pageant, or so I was convinced Liza thought.

The phone rang, far away, heard but not really at hand. It rang again. I answered.

"You're looking outside, I suppose?" Beth's voice usually sparkled. Now it probed tentatively to sense the direction of my plans.

"Hey, how about 'hello darling,' or something old-fashioned and corny like that?" I said, buying time as I stared outside. Like a giant snow scene observed through the murky glass of my office window (the window-washers hadn't been there since July), the downtown was immersed in white. Swirling, gusting, spraying eddies of snow made it all appear as if an unseen hand had picked the glass ball up, shaken it, and set it down again.

"Don't be cute," Beth rejoined. "You're not going, are you?"

"Well, actually, down here it's not so bad . . . it's wet at least."

"I was afraid of that. Who do you think you're kidding? But you're not taking Joey?" So much was encompassed in her question. She knew danger was involved. No well-intended, or not so well-intended, deception on my part could change that.

"Look, I'll be home in a half hour or so. We'll talk about it then."

"I mean it. I don't want you to go. And I really don't want Joey to go."

By ten that morning I was at home, bundling Joey into a snow suit which would be too warm after five minutes on the road. The gesture was meant more for Beth's peace of mind than Joey's protection from the cold. Beth stood in the doorway to the kitchen, saying little. As I moved the zipper upwards on Joey's coat, Beth found her voice.

"Can I see you in the kitchen for a moment?"

"But Joey's all dressed . . ."

"I said for a moment." Her voice was taut.

I left Joey stranded on the rug of the family room and followed Beth into the kitchen.

"Okay, look," I began, "I know how you feel . . ."

"No, you don't. Or you wouldn't go. I think this is dumb. Really dumb. And I'm mad. But I don't want you to leave thinking that I don't understand what you're going through."

"Beth, I'm sorry, but . . ."

"I'm almost finished. I just want you to remember how precious Joey and you both are to me. For God's sake be careful. Pull over if it gets too slick. Call me if you get into trouble. I'll stay around here."

Joey had risen up with his burden of cloth and quilting and staggered into the kitchen after us.

"Go see Liza, Daddy?" Joey asked.

"Yes, buddy, yes . . . I think so."

The last three words were spoken with an eye on Beth, my only concession to her anger and concern, and to the reality I observed out the back window. Snow had begun to layer and obscure the black limbs of the giant oak trees which stood sentinel over the yard.

"I love you. Both of you. Have a good trip." Her words ceased. There was more to say, but no use in saying it.

I leaned over and kissed her, flashed what on reflection was a foolish grin, and picked up my boy in my arms. Beth stepped back, her arms folded, biting her lower lip. Her anger had at least subsided. Her humor began to return.

"I hate it when you get that goofy John Wayne look about you. It happens when it snows and I don't like it. It's really dangerous out there."

"I know," I said. And I really did. I had driven the two and a half miles from the office to home. If it was bad in the city, it would be worse in the country. Yet I stubbornly plodded forward with my plan.

I kissed Beth again at the front door, told her I would call from Cincinnati, carefully watched her face as she kissed Joey, then bundled him and his teddy bear into the child seat next to me. We were on our way.

The freeway was deceptively clear. We circled the city going east and north, then turned onto the expressway heading due north. In a matter of moments I realized that the weather was definitely worse in the country. With an odd sense of detachment I marveled at the perfectly calibrated changes taking place each two or three miles further along. Traffic sloshed along at sixty, then fifty-five, then fifty, and finally settled down to the grating but seemingly safe speed of forty-five miles per hour. In perfect synchronism with the traffic, the left-hand lane slowly transformed from blacktop highway to gray roadway to a narrow white path, tire tracks becoming more visible as I drove onward. Finally, the left lane gave out completely and I surrendered it to semis and hell-for-leather fools in Lincolns and Cadillacs and LTD's.

Joey raised his chin and perused the strange, white world about him, showing no outward fear, but exhibiting more quiet than usual. His two-year-old prattle had trailed off like the left-hand lane of the expressway. The snow had effectively silenced both of us.

"I love you, Joey," I told him, feeling for the first time the fear of sliding toward death. It was a fear I should have felt before leaving.

"Go see Liza?" he asked, his eyes not on me, but the rolling hills and woods which were slowly darkening, though it wasn't quite noon.

"Yes, buddy, we're going to see Liza." There was no sense of self-congratulation or bravado in my voice. I had probably made the wrong decision and I knew it. But my choice had been made. It was harder to turn back than to go on.

Mile after mile we paraded in the right lane, caught in a plodding cavalcade of cars which had little alternative but to follow the slowest. I gripped the steering wheel with both hands. My comments to Joey were short and seldom. My eyes were fixed on the car in front of me. My body tensed, conscious of every vibration from the road, every slight shimmy of the tires. The snow shot into my windshield, playing 3-D games with my sense of the road. I had driven long distances in blizzards that were worse. I had careened off of the road on trips home from school. But I had never carried a child's life with my own on such a venture.

The radio was on, but as the reception grew faint near the mid-point between Louisville and Cincinnati, I became afraid to release my grip on the wheel to change the station. Static ruled for several miles until I reached over like a man disarming a bomb and shoved a tape into place. As far as I was concerned, *Perry Como's Christmas Album* could play over and over from that point until we reached Cincinnati. Perry filled the silence more calmly than anything else I could have chosen.

In my rear-view mirror I could see a long line of tractor-trailers approaching in the left-hand lane. Tension moved a notch closer to fear. I turned my wipers to high. Visibility out of my front window was decreasing with the last evidences of pavement even in the right-hand lane. The trucks would make it worse. They would shake my compact car, testing its balance in the snow, then coat it with slush, reducing my visibility to a gray haze.

The first truck approached and began to pass. I gauged the distance between myself and the car in front, ready to drive blindly for fifty yards or so. My worst expectations were met. The wipers barely spread the first wave of slush aside as the second semi was upon us. It passed and I slowed down, less space remaining of the windshield than before.

The third truck stalked us. The car began to shake in the buffeting draft, encased in its frosting of ice and snow. I lost the knowledge of union with the road. Then it happened, coming inevitably, like a nightmare.

We crossed a bridge, or the temperature dropped a degree, transforming the road to ice, or the truck's force destroyed our tentative balance, or I simply lost control. The result was the same. The car started weaving, parting for the first time from the friendly tracks of the cars that had traveled before it. The last, lingering sense of control left my hands. The car was no longer under my command. Sliding as in slow motion, the car careened leftward across the tracks of the offending trucks. I tried ineffectually to turn my wheels the other way. Softly, almost comically, my car continued on its diagonal path across the left shoulder and into the median. We thrashed through snow and dead brush, side-swiped a mile marker, then came to rest.

"Are we there, Daddy?" Joey asked.

I felt more like crying than answering, but I was too happy that we were both alive. I laughed.

"Not by a long shot, Joey!" Unruffled, Perry Como never missed a beat.

I unhooked my seat belt and got out, looking around, but noticing little. Dazed and shaking, I guessed that someone would call the police on his CB radio. Perhaps they already had. Time might have been suspended or flown forward for all I knew at the moment. I was sure that our trip was over. Christmas had abruptly seen an adjustment in our family's schedule.

Then, with the passage of a minute or two, I focused more on the sights and sounds around me. In the shimmering white curtain separating myself from the road, a figure appeared and came toward us. He was a bulky giant of a man in a heavy, red plaid shirt. Behind him his tractor-trailer spread out like an ugly slug on the shoulder of the expressway. Was this the man who almost killed us? In my confusion I failed to realize the impossibility of my thought. Maybe we had forced him off the road. I was readying myself for that accusation with my best lawyer-like calm when he spoke.

"Saw you lose control. I was back a ways. You okay?"

His reddish beard was already filled with icy crystals. Breath rolled from his lips in bursts of white mist. An immense torso was strapped within broad, bright scarlet suspenders.

"Santa Claus! Santa Claus!" I could hear Joey crying out from the front seat.

"Well, I'll be damned," he said. "I didn't even see the little guy."

Joey's head was craned upwards and to the side, watching us as we stood in the median talking. The trucker made a goofy face and waved to Joey. Joey smiled.

"So," he repeated, "you all okay?"

"I guess," I said after a moment's thought. "They ran us off the road."

"Well," he rubbed his bare hands together and blew on them for warmth. "I didn't see the whole thing. Maybe you're right. Point is, this is crappy weather to be out driving."

His simple comment diffused my anger, reminding me that I was in part to blame for even being on the highway. I nodded.

"You're right. Can you call for help or something?"

"Tell you what. Get in your car and I'll give you a push. It's pretty level here and it don't look like you damaged nothing."

The option of continuing our little pilgrimage had not occurred to me. Our unsolicited savior was right. With a little help we might be able to go on.

I jumped into the car and turned on the ignition. The engine turned over twice and caught. The big man moved to the rear of the car and I rolled my window down so that I could hear him.

"I'll push until you get traction and can get your car to the shoulder. Give me a chance to get back in the rig. Then follow me. These eighteen-wheelers break up the ice pretty good."

"That's a deal. Thanks!" I shouted.

Those were the last words we exchanged. He leaned over and lent his weight to my back bumper. I hadn't asked his name. I never thought to get his license. One of his trucking fraternity had contributed to our departure from the road and now he had appeared to ease our return. It was that simple. It was, I supposed, part of the code.

As we nudged back onto the expressway, the trucker leading the way, Joey turned to me, his eyes wide open and questioning.

"Go see Liza, Daddy?"

"I hope so, Joey. I hope so."

I had no idea whether we would reach Cincinnati in time or in one piece. I knew that it would take longer to turn back and might be just as dangerous. I knew that we might still make Liza's Christmas pageant. Or we might not. I knew that I was no wiser nor my judgment more sound than when we began.

I tried not to glance at the quartz clock on the dashboard, its little staccato strokes ticking off the seconds on the road. It was 12:30. The pageant would start at 1:30. We were still fifty miles from Cincinnati and another five miles thereafter from Liza's school. I followed the semi as a mariner follows the north star, letting his eighteen wheels grind the snow and ice ahead. Joey played with his bear, serenely sucking his thumb, assuming all the while that everything would happen whenever we arrived, regardless of the time. We followed and I was happy to be safer. Time would simply pass. We would arrive when we could.

Eventually the countryside became suburban, then commercial, and finally shopping centers and cinemas marked our approach to the city. Our unnamed, flannel-shirted friend turned off the highway. He had led us well through the ice and snow. I honked my horn and Joey waved. Then he was gone.

The snow no longer obscured the northbound lanes, but patches of ice made them nearly as treacherous. It was 1:15. I gripped the wheel and quietly hoped we might make it. I could see the skyline of the city through the man-made gap cut thirty years before.

We started down that last steep incline to the Ohio River and the city. I turned just long enough to smile at Joey. A tightening of his lip, a slight widening of his eyes, something made me turn around again and simultaneously begin to brake. Where a moment before the traffic was moving, it now stood still. In the distance, not fully comprehended in that instant, a car had panicked, braked, and been struck from the rear. I swerved, not believing that twice in one trip it could happen. My tires hit dry pavement. The car lurched, then righted itself. The driver behind me honked his horn and gestured at me, but we avoided the pileup.

Once we reached the interstate bridge, the traffic cleared. At the state line the expressway seemed miraculously to rid itself of offending ice. I increased our speed and hastened towards Liza's school. Our journey was over, and with it, our time. It was 1:30. I wound up through the old neighborhood where Liza's school awaited us, and the streets turned on us again. The worn bricks from the era of horses and wagons accepted varying degrees of ice and snow, and each square foot offered a different texture. The car stuttered in and out of control. Liza's ancient schoolhouse loomed ahead in spent Gothic splendor.

I eased the car to the curb and turned my wheels toward the sidewalk. We had gotten lucky and were directly across the street from the school. For the first time in over three hours I felt truly safe. I needed just a moment. It wouldn't matter so much now. We were late, but we would be there for Liza during the pageant, and when it was over.

"That's Liza's school," I told Joey. He thrust his small body forward, straining to escape the shoulder straps which had kept him from harm. "Let's get our stuff together. Then we'll go."

I imagined how moments before Liza had chafed within the green stucco walls of her classroom, waves of steam heat passing over her, squirming in her time-worn school seat, certain that her father would arrive any minute. Certain that before the pageant began, he would come strolling down the arched, catacomb-like halls with Joey in his arms, ready to see her perform, then take her home for Christmas. There was no question that he would arrive. Like the intrepid Magi of old, he would enter on cue with a gift of love far greater than any material baggage he might carry along. For Liza, as for Joey, there had never been a question about danger, or turning back, or death. There was no question in their minds that I was all-knowing, wise, and capable of any undertaking.

Sitting behind the steering wheel, however, trying to compose myself, I had my doubts whether anything about my decision had been wise. Stubborn, yes. Loving, yes. Self-confident, at first. But wise? Then, as Joey continued to struggle in his car seat, an odd thought occurred to me. If the Magi had been summarily put to death at King Herod's court for the impertinence of their journey, would history or theology or legend have considered them so wise? Perhaps they too had sensed a need for love to overcome good sense and prudence. In the quiet of that moment, I realized that while I might not share wisdom with the Magi, we were alike driven by a mission of love.

"Okay, Joey, let's go see Liza." I released my little boy and he leaped into my arms. I gathered up my camera, hoisted Joey against my shoulder and clambered out of the car.

"Liza! Liza!" he shouted, pointing across the street. I turned and saw Liza's face pressed against the window of her first floor classroom. As I would find out later, the pageant had been delayed. I can't remember whether it was a microphone that had to be fixed or an item of unfinished business that the principal needed to address. It didn't matter. Like myself, it was late but intact. For Liza and Joey, it was only what had been expected all along.

I hurried across the street and into the school. Liza met us at the door of the classroom. Joey jumped into her arms, sister and brother hugging each other fiercely. Like the Magi of old, I had been lucky, and perhaps like them, my greatest wisdom lay in my knowledge of that fact.

MY DAD'S IDEA
OF CHRISTMAS

Three hundred and thirty-five days or so out of the year my dad's a pretty normal kind of guy. He goes to his office, he comes home and watches the news or reads the paper, we go to baseball games in the spring and summer, and he watches my football games in the fall (I play second string, but he tells me I'm great anyway). Life generally rolls along normally from the middle of January to about Thanksgiving. Then it happens: the fifth season of the year—Christmas.

You see, that's what it is for Dad. It's not just Christmas Day or Christmas week or the Christmas holidays. It's an honest-to-God *season*, like fall or spring or whatever. Now, don't get me wrong. I love Christmas. I can't help it. I come by it naturally. Genetically, even. If I didn't love Christmas, I'd probably be disowned. I'd be "boiled with my own pudding, and buried with a stake of holly through my heart." Yeah, I know where that comes from, Ebenezer. I've known since I was five. I had the equivalent of oral exams every time we watched a Christmas movie or read a Christmas story. There are times when Dad's zeal teeters over into fanaticism. This last Christmas he really worked us all into a frenzy. It was a turning point of sorts, and we'll never forget it.

It all began the day after Thanksgiving, early even for Dad. He started just before dawn that Friday getting all of the decorations out. You're probably thinking, "No big deal. A couple of boxes of lights and maybe a few more boxes of ornaments." Well, think again. That would be the normal person's idea of decorations. Not my dad's. Our family stored lights and ornaments and you name it, like nuclear bomb freaks stored canned goods in their fallout shelters back in the sixties.

Dad hadn't discarded a strand of lights or a pretty run of tinsel since he was five. We had glass ball ornaments that predated the Ark. And if one was ever broken in the process of loading or unloading, it was always his favorite. If it truly *was* one of his favorites, one could hear a string of cuss words that would make Rudolph's nose go off like a rocket. Then Dad would apologize and skulk off to the back hallway and mourn its passing for awhile. Not that a broken ornament wasn't replaced. It was like some Old Testament rule of thumb. Break one. Replace ten.

Mom was pretty strict about the tree lights. She insisted on the small kind that seem to come in strings of a thousand. The kind that go off mysteriously all at once, then relight without warning. They're also the kind that tangle up into knots and graft themselves onto the branches of the tree when you're ready to take it down. But Mom claims they're cooler and safer and daintier, although the constant blinking gives her a headache sometimes.

Dad's preference was and is the kind that he grew up with: big, prominent, hot-burning bulbs that come in a strand of seven or eight. For awhile he quietly fought Mom on the "big versus little light" battleground, but he finally gave up and retreated into putting his lights on the mantel or over a doorway. I must admit, I liked the big lights too, and I've told Dad that. He appreciates an ally every now and then.

Well, last year *all* of the paraphernalia came out the day after Thanksgiving. Not in increments or at all selectively. Dad just brought it all out and stacked it in six-foot columns throughout the back hall. He seemed possessed by the Christmas spirit, not simply aglow with it. That weekend we decorated everything *but* the Christmas tree. Even Dad knew that a live, cut tree—or I guess I should say, a dead, cut tree—won't keep until Christmas if you buy it before the first or second weekend in December. But even without the tree, there was still plenty to do—every room, every mantel in our old Victorian house, every doorway, every light fixture. There was enough to keep us busy.

The next weekend we bought the tree. Dad seemed to be stepping up everything, making it earlier, bigger and, I guess he thought, better. It was a beautiful tree—at least eight-and-a-half feet tall—and, as usual, my dad swelled with self-satisfaction as he negotiated five dollars off the price. Secretly I think we all supposed the guys at the haymarket saw Dad coming and jacked the price up ten dollars, but we acted as if he had really driven the bargain hard. We rode home in triumph with our carcass secured fast to the luggage carrier. Dad and I got it in the stand, balanced it, and wired it at the top as an extra precaution. Then we sat down for lunch, and Dad dropped his bombshell.

"Honey, I thought we'd trek up to Cincinnati next weekend, spend the day shopping, grab a bite to eat and come home Saturday night." My dad set his coffee mug down with solemn resolve. The pilgrimage to Cincinnati was a key part of our Christmas celebration. Cincinnati was Dad's home city—even though he grew up across the river in Kentucky. And for Dad it was the holy city of American Christmas celebrations. Its downtown was like no other. Store windows were filled with moving toy figures. Pogue's Arcade was a winter wonderland of lights and artificial snow. For my little sister, and years before for me, there wasn't just one, but two Santa's Toy Lands to visit. Cincinnati on a Saturday in December was a heaven on earth—or so my father saw it.

"Well," my mother started tentatively, a hint of dissent in her voice, "we've got the open house at the Armstrong's and . . ."

"You hate that open house . . . too many drunks." My dad was waiting for her. "I think next weekend would be perfect," my dad repeated with a big Burt Lancaster grin. He was trying to be good-natured but firm.

"But Dad . . ." I knew as I spoke those two simple words that my intonation would give me away. I enjoyed our annual trip to Cincinnati at Christmas . . . most years. Cincinnati's shopping district always made you feel that an old-fashioned, downtown, hustle and bustle Christmas was more than just a scene from an old movie. Bright lights, car horns honking, window displays, no tacky shopping centers. There was the comforting feel of being blanketed by old buildings, all warm and cheery. But the following Saturday was not a good choice on Dad's part.

"But if we don't go this weekend, Tad," his voice had softly modulated into his I-can-be-reasonable-about-this tone, "we won't be able to go at all."

"Dad, let's not go at all!" Molly squealed. I winced. The girl had no subtlety about her. All she remembered was the seemingly endless hours of shopping just one year before. I sunk down in my chair. Mom instinctively moved closer to her in a protective mode, though Dad has never raised anything but his voice, always chickening out of any corporal punishment that was promised.

"Now, darling," Dad was always sweet with Molly. "It will be fun. They have toy displays and whole tables full of trains and pretty decorations and . . ." Dad knew how to play his hand, "Santa Claus!"

"Yippee!" Molly screamed. Dad had quickly bribed her into a state of forgetfulness. Last year's boredom was suddenly a distant memory.

"But Dad . . ." I couldn't help myself. "I've already made a date with Sarah Jane. If I break it, that's it, she'll go out with Dirk the Neanderthal." And I was serious. Maybe hormones were outracing my common sense, but it was *the* date of my limited and recent love life, and Dirk was, in most respects, merely humanoid. I don't mean to get off the subject, but as nice a girl as Sarah Jane McCarthy was, she would go out with monosyllabic Dirk just because he asked her out . . . and was an All-State tight end. And he would exact more kisses from Sarah Jane in one hour than I would dare accomplish all fall. But I had learned not to question such luck. It was simply the law of the jungle, skillfully to be circumvented whenever possible.

Dad looked at me, steadier now, more rationally. I stared back intensely. "Come on, Dad," I was trying to tell him with my eyes, "you've been there. You know what will happen if I break this date."

"I'll tell you what, Tad," he said with a slow I've-got-the-answer grin, "We'll just ask Sarah Jane to go with us."

"Oh, no!" my soul silently screamed, my lips impassive. Asking Sarah Jane McCarthy to go with us would be worse than my junior high dances where Mom or Dad taxied me to a date. The vision of having Sarah Jane squeezed between Molly and me in the back seat of the Ford was nearly as bad as the vision of Sarah Jane squeezed between Dirk Broadhead and the passenger door of his father's Audi. You notice I said "nearly as bad."

"Okay . . ." I forced a grin, "but let's get back to town as early as possible . . ."

Later that day I called Sarah Jane, gulped only once, and tried to be upbeat about a date with my entire family. Something or other must have been wrong, because she acted really excited about the idea. She went on about how her family never went on fun trips like that and how she'd never spent any time shopping in downtown Cincinnati and how she thought my dad was really fun to be with and Molly was the cutest little sister ever! I couldn't believe what I was hearing, but I didn't question. The date was set and she was safe, for the moment, from Dirk and his 42-inch reach.

"Why don't you invite Sarah Jane over for breakfast Saturday morning?" Mom suggested out of the blue. I thought for a second and realized it was a wonderful idea. I'd never had breakfast with a girl—I don't count Molly, of course—and there was something, well, sexy about it. No, that's not the right word. I don't know exactly what I mean. Anyway, I thought it was a great idea.

"Gee, that's a great idea," I repeated out loud. That was still my general assessment by the time I sprung the idea on Sarah Jane. She thought it would be a perfect way to start the day. I could pick her up at nine, we'd have breakfast at my house and head off for Cincinnati.

It was only then that I started having second thoughts. She didn't know my family all that well. Everything she had said on the phone about them was based on a few meetings at school and once or twice at the swimming pool. She had never been submitted to Father Christmas for twelve hours or been subject to Molly's silly questions for an eternity. I was riding the roller coaster of teen love, heading for a dip as the week passed. What I couldn't foresee was that the dip would continue.

"Tad . . ." I was completely attentive at the mere whisper of my name by Sarah Jane. Since we were in third period English, Sarah Jane's whisper was very quiet indeed. Mrs. Rutabush might be old enough to have taught my mother, but she had the ears of a jackal.

"Tad, Dirk has invited us over to his house on Saturday night to play games and listen to some new CDs. A bunch of the guys on the team are going to be there, and he thought it would be fun."

My blood went cold. Fun. Little did she know. One must remember that I had been in a huddle or two with Dirk Broadhead. His idea of fun was either tearing the wings off of flies or sacking and pillaging. I was instantaneously thrust into a triple dilemma. If I said no to Dirk's generous invitation, I would seem jealous or scared of the competition. I was both. If the journey to Cincinnati lasted too long, I was convinced that my family's charm would wear very thin on Sarah Jane, and I would never see her again. If we did get home in time to go to the party, Dirk would find some way of hustling Sarah Jane into the den while I was detained by some of my so-called teammates. There could be no victory. I acceded, just as Mrs. Rutabush wheeled about and enforced silence upon us.

When Saturday arrived I had an awful time trying to figure out just how I felt. I spent far too much time last year trying to figure out how I felt, and Saturday was typical of my excess. Nevertheless, I decided that a flawed date with Sarah Jane was better than no date at all.

Breakfast went more smoothly than I expected. Mom must have drugged Molly. She was polite, but charming, precocious, but never

obnoxious. Dad was even better. This man, who had so often con-
ducted himself at Christmas time with the subtlety of Chevy Chase,
was suddenly a suave and debonair Michael Caine. No goofing off.
No singing Bing Crosby Christmas songs over the pancakes (not
"White Christmas," mind you. He sings the theme song from the
"Bells of St. Mary's"). No tickling Molly or Mom. He had the poise
of a *G.Q.* model.

Of course, this threw me into a false sense of security. We got
into the car, got onto the expressway, and headed off for the Valhalla
of retailing religiosity. I was soaring. Everything would be all right.
My imagination ran wild. My fantasies took flight.

Mom and Dad would quietly secret Molly off, setting a time for
Sarah Jane and me to meet them. Then Sarah Jane and I could wander
off, walk around Fountain Square and maybe even take a carriage
ride. I was my father's son, and while not nearly as corny as my
dad, I was every bit as romantic.

My dreams developed hairline fissures halfway up the road and
huge gaps right before we started the last stretch towards Christmas
City. It started with Molly. She was so excited about having Sarah
Jane present that she wouldn't leave her alone. It was yap, yap, yap
the whole way. My little sister, who didn't have a dozen words for
me in any given day, was reeling off rapid-fire questions and inter-
spersed monologue for Sarah Jane. Then there was the matter of the
radio.

Now, Dad's not an easy-listening nerd. He knows almost as much
about rock as I do—and a bit more about the old rock stars. Usually
we have no fights over the right station. But, of course, this was
Christmas. So the radio was replaced by taped Christmas classics of
the last forty years. Dad hadn't even gotten the selections he was
playing from the late night mail order commercials. He had made
this tape up himself. And was it corny! Bing Crosby and Perry Como
and Nat King Cole and Frank Sinatra. They would have lasted all
the way to Cleveland, let alone Cincinnati.

Finally, there was the little matter of altered plans. There we were,
ten miles outside of the big dream downtown. I could practically
see—and even feel—myself cuddled under a blanket with Sarah Jane,
trotting around the old German-built city, jingle bells tinkling, Sal-
vation Army bells ringing, when my father suddenly had a flash.

"You know, we've got time . . . let's take a spin through my old
hometown, get a snack at the Briar Cliff Drug Store . . . say 'hi' to
some of my old buddies we'll see." In one sentence he had delayed
my realization of teenage ecstasy by at least two hours.

"But Dad," I fumbled for something . . . some key phrase that would redirect him. "Dad, won't it be too late to shop if we take any more time?" It was the best I could do under pressure.

"Why, it's only 1:30 now. We'll be in downtown in a couple of hours . . . just right for seeing the lights, catching a couple of hours shopping, a bite to eat and then home." Finality tinged his voice. There was no further discussion to be had.

So back we went to Dad's hometown. It was like I read in an old novel Dad had picked up at a used bookstore: "Last night I dreamt I went to Manderley again." The gradual ascent to the little bedroom community nestled on the Kentucky hillside overlooking the Ohio River, the familiar street names long ago incorporated into my dad's private mythology, and the certain houses or stores which Dad remembered from his youth. It was kind of nostalgic, I guess you'd say . . . until he got hit with a triple whammy. The first was the old drugstore. Some chain outfit had taken it over and from the outside looking in, it appeared as one colorless flash of bare fluorescent light.

"I used to buy phosphates there," Dad said softly.

"All things have their day." My mom was trying to be upbeat.

"Come back and buy it, and we'll tear out the crappy lights and put the fountain back in." I could hardly believe it was my voice. My dad got a big grin on his face and grabbed my shoulder. I got embarrassed—I admit it. I didn't know what to say.

Well, anyway, from there we drove by Dad's favorite overlook—his hometown seemed to have a dozen knobby hillsides with great views of the river valley—and the house he had dreamed of living in as a kid. You might have guessed. Victorian had yielded to condos on stilts. Some developer must have made a killing. This time no one said a word.

At least the restaurant he took us to for lunch was still standing—but the family who had owned it when Dad was my age was long gone. The food was good, but a dozen or so of the locals must have been in and out while we were there, and Dad didn't know any of them.

"Well, so much for memory lane." Dad finished his coffee and grinned. He had taken it pretty well, I guess. Through it all Molly kept talking to Sarah Jane. They were taking it in stride. Mom was keeping up a good front about a less than perfect afternoon. But I don't know, somehow Dad's sense of the past had rubbed off on me. I knew exactly what he was feeling, and I wanted to say something that would make it okay.

"Well, Dad, let's go on into town. I want to see the lights, get some shopping done . . . what do you say?"

Dad looked at me and he knew that I was right there with him.

Like I said before, I'm my father's son, and while he drives me nuts sometimes, we don't have to say very much to share our thoughts and feelings.

"Okay." He smiled, a smile far more comforting than his forced grin a moment before. "We're on our way."

That was the turning point for me. It was almost four o'clock, and I was really ready for a little bit of old-fashioned, downtown Christmas. We tumbled back into the car, bid the old hometown a farewell of mixed sentiments, and wasted no more time evading our prime target.

Fifteen minutes later we were across the bridge and working our way west on Fourth Street. Buildings loomed on either side of us. Maybe it was the fact that the streets were narrower than at home, but it really was like a big city. We parked next to this big old Gothic church — Dad would never pay to park if he could avoid it — and charged off like miners for the mother lode.

"Not so fast . . . I can't keep up." Mom was the first to point out that we were practically jogging.

"I wouldn't mind a little window shopping along here." Sarah Jane was establishing a kinship of the slow afoot with Mom. That was a good sign.

"I like running in the cold," Molly chirped.

Dad was barely listening. He was leaning into the wind and heading for the Arcade and his favorite old department store. Christmas was about to be fulfilled. Everything thereafter would simply be icing.

"I'm with you, Dad, but maybe we could slow it down a notch."

"We're almost there . . ." His breath puffed out, and he looked like a little steam engine.

"Great," I persisted, a sense of gallantry for Sarah Jane and Mom prompting me with every step, "then let's take it easy."

Dad straightened up and turned around to the rest of us. "Okay. Okay. If you all can't keep up, I can cooperate." Dad could afford magnanimity. We were almost there.

The corner was nearly upon us. Fourth and Vine. The most magical, beautiful block or two in midwestern Christmasdom was about to light up before us. Dad rushed ahead. We couldn't stop him. I was close at his heels. Molly, Mom and Sarah Jane were in a cluster ten feet behind. We were within a few feet of our destination.

When I got to Dad, I wondered for an instant why he was stopped at a green crosswalk sign. But only for an instant. I could hear Mom's words behind me.

"Oh . . . my . . . God."

My sentiments exactly. I looked up the street. Were we at the right block? Yes, no doubt about it. We were exactly where we had set out to arrive earlier in the day . . . and even the week before when Dad first announced the pilgrimage. But *where* we had set out to arrive no longer possessed *what* we had come to see. My father's—and, all moaning and groaning aside—the family's favorite department store was simply no more. No brightly lit window displays, no fantasy-like arcade, no high arching department store entrance ways—no building at all. Just an empty, ugly, gloomy hole in the ground, encircled by some shabby wire fencing.

A minute can be a long time when you actually stop to count the seconds. I'm sure no one spoke for a full minute.

"Did they move it somewhere?" Molly was the first to break the pall.

"No, darling," mother noted gently, "they just tore it down and threw it away."

Molly's mouth opened in amazement. "They threw away Christmas?" she asked.

This was too much. You can save your old ornaments and lights or pack away the treasured stories and Bing Crosby records, but you can't keep a city from tearing itself down. Two generations of us stood heartsick, mourning a once grand building, my Dad's Christmas Mecca now reduced to rubble.

"That's somebody's idea of progress," Dad stated at last. "Not my idea . . . but somebody's."

"Well, it's not like they knew we were coming." Sarah Jane's addition was meant to console. And she was right. What business of it was ours? We don't even pay taxes in Ohio.

"You're right, Sarah Jane," Dad said. "Let's all take a walk around the block."

Well, our walk was about as zippy as a funeral procession. The fountain at the Square was at least assurance that downtown hadn't been the victim of some cruel war that had shelled the Ohio side of the river but left Kentucky untouched. It's a public place and relatively safe from that sort of thing. But the pretty lights there just didn't make up for the loss we all felt. I mean, there's just something nostalgic about the tradition of retailing and overdone decorations and jostling people and bright packages filled with things that will be returned by their new owner the day after Christmas. It was a short, silent stroll around the block, and when it was over we were ready to exit the one-time preserve of my dad's dreams and memories.

Without a peep, we automatically started back for the car. It was getting dark and by my past calculations, Sarah Jane and I should have been snuggled beneath a blanket in a carriage, driven by the cold to mutual warmth. For some reason I was at the lead point of our little troop, having all but forgotten any would-be gallantry. I got to the car first, but Dad had the keys, so I had to wait for everybody to catch up. I can't explain exactly what happened next. Somehow, as I look back on it, it seems as if a lot more was really going on than you would think for the short amount of time it took to happen. I looked over at the church—some big, old Episcopal church—and heard the most beautiful organ music coming out of the opened doors. Inside the lights were low, and I even saw the flickering of some candles through the stained glass. People were filing into the church at a pretty good pace. This much I took in before my dad reached the car.

I saw him look at the church—more than just a quick glance—and look back at me. He never said a word, and we're Presbyterians, not Episcopalians, anyway, so it wasn't like it was the absolutely obvious thing to do. But his eyes seemed to ask a question. "What do you think, Tad? Should we take another chance or call it quits?"

Surely as if those words were spoken, they registered and I stepped back. Dad wasn't telling me—he was asking me. He was asking *me* what *I* thought. He was making me a partner as well as a son. I thought for a second, shocked but excited, then nodded in agreement. "You bet, Dad," I thought. My dad smiled and stood up straight.

"I think we should visit this church," he said, ". . . it says right here on the gate 'All Welcome', and I'll bet they mean it."

Sarah Jane and Mom looked a little surprised, but they quickly went along. Molly floored all of us.

"All right!" she let out in glee, which is really odd, because Molly's your typical squirmy little kid in church and usually gripes and complains every Sunday morning.

Well, we walked right in, the ushers smiling at us just like we belonged. And you know, I guess, we did. I'd always thought of churches and their sects like little non-exclusive but well-defined "clubs" which one might occasionally visit but could never belong to. But on that late Saturday afternoon two weeks before Christmas, we actually belonged. We might never come back, but it didn't matter. When the organ accompanied everyone in a hymn, when the choir marched up the aisle, and even when they and the head minister presented the show and pageant or whatever it was, we belonged. And I guess because of that we all got a little weepy during the organ finale and the last hymn. Even Dad, smiling as goofy as could be, sang out like he was an alum of the choir. His eyes were all watery and he kept sniffling as if the cold had gotten to him, but I knew he was trying not to cry. I guess I was trying, too. And in that moment

I felt as close to Dad as I ever had. Mom was standing beside us and about that time she squeezed my hand. I looked and saw her holding Dad's with her other hand. Funny how she must have known as well.

We filed out, thanked everybody for letting us visit, and sniffed and blinked as the cold hit our noses and chilled our tears. We took a collective breath, exhaled steamy mist about us, started to pile into the car, then sighted a dinky little German restaurant across the street. "Let's go in," I said, and go in we did.

I suppose I could go on, but I'll wind down instead. The food was fine, the waiters were funny, and there were even candles on our table. Somebody played Christmas carols on an accordion. Sarah Jane snuggled close to me in the booth we had all piled into, and kissed me once when no one was looking. I didn't worry about Dirk the football jock all evening. In fact, the whole thing was just great.

But you know, the really important thing wasn't what we did or where we went or how we swore we'd do it again. The important thing was that my dad—my good old, preachy, overly traditional dad—had been graced with a new idea of Christmas, and the idea wasn't just his, but mine and Mom's and Sarah Jane's and even Molly's. It didn't depend on any particular church or city or state; it wasn't even a new idea, exactly. But somehow we'd never thought of it in the same way as decorations and department stores. Most of all, it was pretty safe from city fathers, immune from hot-shot developers, and more durable than bricks and mortar. This idea of Christmas would be there when Dad's old seven-per-strand bulbs burned out and the Bing Crosby records finally broke. No, come to think of it, they hadn't torn Christmas down and thrown it away after all.